THE CROOKED THING

Caitlin Press Inc.
8100 Alderwood Road,
Halfmoon Bay, BC V0N 1Y1
www.caitlin-press.com

Text and cover design by Vici Johnstone
Edited by Arleen Paré
Printed in Canada

Caitlin Press Inc. acknowledges financial support from the Government
of Canada and the Canada Council for the Arts, and the Province of
British Columbia through the British Columbia Arts Council and the
Book Publisher's Tax Credit.

Library and Archives Canada Cataloguing in Publication
Crooked thing : stories / by Mary MacDonald
MacDonald, Mary, author.
Canadiana 20200224131 | ISBN 9781773860312 (softcover)
LCC PS8625.D657 C76 2020 | DDC C813/.6—dc23

The Crooked Thing

Stories

Mary MacDonald

CAITLIN PRESS 2020

Contents

II — Bend to Love

To those I love and those I grieve. And to the light that binds us.

O love is the crooked thing,
There is nobody wise enough,
To find out all that is in it

—W.B.Yeats

I

Love's Long Contour

Under every grief & pine
Runs a joy with silken twine

—William Blake

LE CHAPEAU

"Paris has a child, and the forest has a bird; the bird is called the sparrow; the child is called the gamin." —*Les Miserables*

I Sparrow

I was born into the chaos of WWI. After the war ended, I lived in captivity. Now, in my last years, I have unexpectedly found my home and refuge in a common rose bush in the square de l'Archevêché located behind the Cathédrale de Notre-Dame in Paris. This is, without a doubt, where I belong.

I was in Lille in the north, when our entire flock was displaced. The shrubs, thickets, grasses and ferns where we made our home were trampled and transformed into muddy trenches. My mother died trying to protect our nest. In shock, I took to the air, heading south. I didn't know where to go. By chance, following the coast, I came to the great river Seine and made my way to Paris.

Within the year, I was captured, to be sold for my feathers. People were crazy after the war. Spending money and demanding outlandish clothing. Feathers were sewn into hats for the wealthy while the people of Paris lined up in the streets for food.

At last now, I have found an ordinary life. Simple, safe and free. I have all that I need. There is a certain comfort surviving on the edge of things. Before I die, I have a debt to repay. Until then, a piece of my heart will be missing.

II   Madame

Beneath my bed, stored in a round hatbox, is *un chapeau de regret*. A hat of feathers I made for myself before the war. It is of incredible beauty: black panne velvet with ostrich feathers surrounding the brim that I made to dance. More lavish than a single plume. I embroidered each one with a care *extraordinaire*. The round brim turned, just so, to sit low over the eye. I was employed in the salon of Madame Vionnet on the Rue de Rivoli. All eyes were on Paris. We made copies of the hats of Coco Chanel. It was a booming and exciting time. But something beautiful can become painful. Later, the eyes, wings, and in some cases, entire bodies of birds were carefully arranged onto the hats. These birds had been slaughtered or died of starvation. I have heard tell that in America the selling of rare birds for feathers has been outlawed now. The same law will surely pass in France. We have committed atrocities. Now, so soon after the war, it is unthinkable that we carry on the same.

III   Sparrow

I am at her window on the *6ème étage*. The light on the Île Saint-Louis is spectacular this time of day. Golden and dreamy in a way that lifts my burdens, at least for a while. The zinc rooftop is hot. Too hot for my old and fragile feet. I notice the pigeons have all taken shelter too. Autumn this year has been unusually warm, the days as hot as mid-summer. I shuffle under the dormer until I am cool. Then I settle quietly and watch. One must be still when gathering impressions. It is absolutely her I am staring at. My throat swells with anticipation; there is no question. I have longed for this moment, but never believed it would come. Studying faces for so many years. Flying from *quartier* to *quartier*. There were always people in the streets and parks, walking or lingering in groups, or in the cafés talking. I would alight on a table, the tip of a fence or partition, the long-rounded edge of the bar, and listen. But their stories did not interest me. I was waiting for her.

In the thin light this late afternoon, she sits on a low wooden stool in her millinery, her slim fingers pull a needle though a piece of felt as though it was silk. The concentration of the kind a mother has for her baby. I wish she were my mother. Her fingers would sweep my feathers until all my sorrowful memories vanished. The bones of her back are rounded and poke through her jumper, like a skeleton. *Are you well?* Parisians have been hungry. I notice the wooden beams of the *atelier* are spotless of cobwebs and dust. There is a single bed against the wall and a basin. A cupboard with wooden head forms, threads, beads, buttons, pearls, bottles of glue, pins, rolls of string, ribbon, lace and fabric, and in the corner a stack of boxes.

There are no feathers in her *atelier*. Many birds were slaughtered for making hats. Exotic birds more beautiful than I am. Almost my fate too. I am shivering, even in this heat, and have to grapple with the ledge to keep from falling. I am a little *joyeux* and a little *triste* at the same time. Which is strange now that I've found her. I want to fly in through the open window. I want to fly to her shoulder. But stop myself. That is too bold.

The recognition was instant when I saw her depart the Boulangerie des Deux Ponts this morning. My eyes are attuned to shiny things. A simple navy *cloche*, gathered on the one side, held with a single silver button. It was the button, caught by the light, I saw first. The stitching was perfect, of course. There would never be feathers in her hat. I was seized by a happiness I cannot explain. I followed her as she walked unsteadily, but without pause, towards the river. When she stopped to look in a shop window, she slumped and looked weary. Then her high-button boots turned and carried on. Clicking on the uneven cobblestones. I wanted to call out to her. *What is your name?*

Many are the nights I woke alone. Frightened, I made flights around the Île. Riding high, dipping low. Waiting. Holding her in my memory. Light lingered like the heat of the day on the rooftops. I did not dream that she was near.

There is a filling up in me. Then a great exhale, and I am crying. I remember my mother saving me by shoving me out of the nest as the tanks caterpillared through. She whispered to me as we parted, singing with her last breath.

IV Madame

One day, *le vent très forte*, I made an excursion to the Marché aux Fleurs on Île de la Cité. It had been hot for many days and I was grateful for the wind and the sound of rain tapping on the metal rooftop of the *atelier* of my millinery when I awoke. I had chosen my route carefully. I wanted to pass by the gypsy encampment. There was a young boy I have seen who plays the banjo. I threw a few coins in his tin can and stopped to listen. Trying to resist my nostalgia for the music that could be heard everywhere before the war. We must begin again. I felt joy listening to this boy filling the streets with his swiftly moving beat, somehow swinging abruptly from happy to sad, from abundance to longing.

It is 1920. The war is only two years over. It has been wonderful to hear music and voices of children again in the streets. Paris will come back to life. Fashion is returning. Working women, like me, are more common now. My hip aches from sitting and my eyes are dull from the demands of my work. I can stitch on bright colours, but the dark ones are tricky. Still, people are starving. I am lucky to be inside; my fingers are warm. There are enough commissions for the winter. There is music playing on the Pont Saint-Louis. And a breeze swaying the linden trees. If I wasn't feeling my age and stubborn as an old mule holding tight to my regrets, I might start dancing.

V Sparrow

I am one of the few free songbirds in Paris. I stretch my neck and shake. I am a simple white-throated sparrow. A passerine. Rare in Western Europe. Not as sought after as heron, ostrich, osprey or egret. Though I was kept in a cage like the others, passed from hand to hand, groped by merchants shopping for feathers. Exotic birds are being imported now from New Guinea, Moluccas, China. Sold at the market. But I am not magnificent, and every day, as the market closed, I was relieved not to have been chosen.

It took me a month to make the journey to Paris. Some days, I was tired, so tired, I can't tell you, and frightened too. I felt I was flying straight off the ends of the earth. One of my wings became shredded and trembled in flight and I fought to stay aloft. I saw the river first and trees golden in sunlight and followed, mesmerized, to the center of this ancient city. I was alone and cold and unsure I would survive the winter.

But Paris was not a stranger to me, as I would have imagined. Rather, it was wonderfully familiar. There were many birds, who shared bread, seeds and suet to build my strength, showed me how to cluster for warmth and sleep beneath niches of Cathédrale de Notre-Dame. I knew nothing of life in the wild except fright and loneliness. Île de la Cité was calm and orderly and I found a kind of peace. A little slice of *paradis*. Until one morning I was netted.

It was a robust woman in large laced boots and red hair tied with a kerchief. I mistook her for a street sweeper and was careless, feeding off the sidewalk on some seeds children had thrown. "You'll have to do," she said. "*Pas mal.*" The next thing I knew, I'd been tossed into a canvas sack and hauled to a warehouse filled with caged birds. My first response was resignation. I had scarcely regained my strength from my long journey. I was placed into a coop with other small birds. I slumped to the ground, my wings began to quiver; I closed my eyes and tried to picture my mother's eyes, the warm folds of her wing, the slippery cone of her beak stuffing grains into mine.

For that entire winter I never left the warehouse except for market day. Every Saturday morning I was taken to the market. And every Saturday evening I was returned to the warehouse unsold. The loss of liberty was painful. The days were long, the nights were longer still.

VI Madame

Across from the Marché aux Fleurs there were cages with exotic birds. I started down the narrow passage, cages of great length on a long table where the seller was calling out, "Egret, ostrich, peacock, ibis, bird of paradise."

I travelled up and down, appraising the creatures, stuffed together so tightly there wasn't room for them to walk around, let alone fly. They were barely able to gasp a breath. At the end of the row I came to a stop. In a *petit cage à oiseaux*, all alone, stood a sparrow so small it must have been newly born. I made a neutral voice. "*Combien pour le petit oiseau?*" I paid the man, grasped the cage, and walked with urgency away from the market. I didn't know where I was going. I walked alongside the Cathédral and straight to square de l'Archevêché, and pushed open a small wooden gate into the garden, the hinge creaking. I did not know what else to do. The bird was making whispering sounds, like it was trying to sing. Then I released the latch and liberated the bird.

VII Sparrow

Soon she puts her work away, tidies the *atelier*. She is on her hands and knees pulling a round hatbox from beneath the bed. Then she reaches for her coat and the navy blue *cloche*. I follow overhead and a short distance behind as she makes an evening stroll along the River Seine, traverses the Pont Saint-Louis. She walks a few metres from my rose bush. Her movements are laboured. The box must be heavy. I have an impression of much sadness in her. *What are you looking for?*

Following her it is possible to see everything from my viewpoint. Couples hand-in-hand, of course. This is Paris. Now, after the sadness of the war, one finds the spirit returning. An eagerness in the air. There is a trio with a cello, a bass and a saxophone on the Pont Saint-Louis and a cigar tin for donations. The rhythm shoots through me with memory; the chorus of my flock. When I was a hatchling, we would sing to each other, as the sun went down. Simply for pleasure. Loss in me echoes louder and louder. I fly high, making the musicians a speck on the ground, and carry on, following *Madame* across the bridge. Now it is twilight. Neither day nor night, but the in-between.

I land on the ledge of the wall adjacent to the river. The space between us is almost nothing. I can hear her breathing. She leans over the balustrade, dropping her forehead toward the river. The strands of her hair cover her face. She is sobbing. Then she removes a hat from the round box. Her body is shaking and I am trembling. *What is this hat?* She flattens the hatbox with her fist.

She begins to tear the hat, piece by piece, feather by feather, releasing the plumes like spent notes, to flutter into the wind and down the river. "I was like a child," she sobs into the evening. "Demanding for myself, the best. *Le plus chic.* Better than all the *grands salons* of Paris." Then she straightens herself, makes a cross on her chest and gathers the box.

I am aghast and find myself rocking back and forth. Yet, watching this scene, so private, I have also witnessed her grace. In the falling light of this autumn evening, we have crossed a bridge together. I had imagined a thousand ways I would meet her. How I would thank her for liberating me. I never imagined an act of this much heartache.

Eventually she heads back the way she came. It is near dark with only a sliver of a new moon to mark the way. I fly around and settle again on my perch under the dormer outside her window and watch as she hangs up her coat, rests her hat on the dresser and lights the lamp. There are but a few metres between us. She moves slowly, sits on the edge of the bed, gazes out the window, staring through me and into the night.

I lift my crown and flick my tail. I flutter my wings, not so much to capture her attention, as to prepare myself. Then I draw in air, making a simple whistle to clear my throat. Up and down to set the pitch. I begin with the lullaby my mother sang to me. *Sleep now sleep, you are not alone.* My eye catches her eye. I raise my voice and continue singing. I have no fear. My voice is a new voice. I am improvising with my own words. Offering my small prayer. *The night is no longer. Our cages have flown.*

ALMOST LIKE LIFE

It's seven o'clock in the morning, an unusual time for a play to begin. Like everyone, before a performance, I'm nervous. A very long show can do that to you. I've arrived alone; I have my ticket and take my seat.

As the curtain opens, the stage lights illuminate a slim person, center stage, dressed in hospital green scrubs and cap, with back to the audience. There is no way to make out if it's a man or a woman. Then turning to face the audience, I see it's a man. It takes me a minute, then I know—I've met this man once. Though I've never seen him in these clothes before. He's the surgeon. The hero in this production.

"We will begin in a few minutes and on time," he speaks directly to the audience. He walks off the stage, so light on his feet, I barely have the sense of having seen him at all. Then the curtain closes. So quickly, I am transported, filled with anticipation and curiosity.

I sit and wait. Nothing begins. I survey my surroundings. I am suddenly in a too cold room waiting for my husband to come out of neurosurgery. The surgery is scheduled to take seven hours. I shift in my chair. I cannot quite settle. It would be nice to look out into the children's garden, the maple trees in mid-June fullness, eavesdropping on young medical students meeting over morning coffee with time to socialize now that exams are done.

But in this waiting room there are no windows. A large vent in the ceiling churns out cold air like the room is an icebox and all the contents must be kept chilled. I'm not wearing a warm enough sweater, my throat is sore and I'm becoming hungry and scared. And the show hasn't begun. The way things are going I'm not going to make it through the whole performance.

I wait two hours and all my plans to sit quietly, attending to the events of the day, suddenly shift like a door slamming shut. An ocean of panic surges and I can barely maintain the self-control to remain in my chair. I have the urge to flee, but I don't. My nerves are too jittery to read a book, listen to music or take a nap. So, I decide to remind myself how brave I can be. I close my eyes and scroll through my memory: I have walked uncommonly long distances, saved disoriented trekkers from the perils of bad weather, pulled sinking youths from mud holes and grieved the loss of family and friends. I can do this too.

I feel a bit like a child who has to tell you things before we begin, so I tell you this. I don't have tusks. You see, once a family has been hunted, the young aren't born with tusks. Apparently, 53 percent of females of my species now are born tuskless. It's not embarrassing exactly. Once you reach adulthood you get over the shock of looking different. Perhaps inconvenient is more accurate. And anyway, there are many of us now.

Tusks are utilitarian more than they are esthetic. In day-to-day life, they are tools for gathering food, excavating for water and fending off predators. But I prefer not to be constantly reminded that I am without defenses. I don't get hung up on all of that. It's also my ace in the hole. People aren't afraid of me. Neither are they expecting me to be heroic.

And what remains unspoken between us? I think that's what we all do when we're waiting. We look around the room. What are you doing here? Though none of us has looked anyone in the eye. There are three other people waiting in this village with me, not including a clerk wearing blue hospital scrubs and a cotton hat covering her hair, sitting at a computer desk behind a half wall. I think it's fair to say from her upright posture and stern manner that she is guarding the door. The door into the recovery room. Which is before the door into the post-op room. And the door after that door. Which I imagine is the door to the operating room. The tension will revolve around that door, which no one can enter without the permission of the clerk.

The curtain opens again and a strange calmness settles in the chilled room. The stage lights focus on one character, a woman, sitting in a corner with a book. She is a small woman with tight grey curls and dressed casually in khaki pants and sandals. Her face, hands and feet are unmoving. We are meant to be looking at her. But why, I wonder. She is facing into the corner and, to my mind, her body closed, wrapped into herself.

I don't think she's reading her book. Her face does not betray any emotions and I have a sense that she's been here before. Even though she isn't moving, there is something happening at a deeper level. The way monks look in meditation. I watch her with interest from the vast Savannah plains where I rise to stand, move and shake my thick and plodding body. I'm here for the first time and the seats are uncomfortably small and flimsy. My mind is not still. Then, as though I have looked away or fallen asleep for an instant, she is suddenly in a tree with her tail wrapped around her. How well monkeys have learned to pass time.

"My wife is having knee surgery. Is she done?"

A man has arrived stage left. Wearing cut-off jeans and flip-flops he walks in like he has stumbled into an open-air bar in the desert. I am surprised by his clothing. Wherever he was before, he is dressed too informally for this setting. He has no interest in the room or in waiting whatsoever. He struts straight to the clerk's desk without looking left or right around the room and begins to pace back and forth in front of the counter. His demeanor signals: I don't belong here.

"Half an hour," the clerk says.

"Half an hour?" He lunges at the clerk. He's all proud head and swept back mane turning towards the lights. He grows even larger and imposing and unleashes a torrent of expletives. "I can't wait a fucking half an hour."

I become protective of the clerk. I'm big too and my size alone is off-putting for most everyone I encounter. And now I see that people can have a brutal manner. Even here, in a hospital. Even here, where we are all waiting, in this very long play. His behaviour is inexcusable and I think the director has made a mistake. I rise up from my chair.

"Here, here."

The clerk catches my eye and signals that she can manage the situation. This is what she knows how to do.

But then I wonder, under his mane and bluster, what? What is underneath?

One thing he does is activate everyone waiting in the room. The guy beside me with earbuds and a black puffy jacket leaps to his feet, knocks back his chair, and charges the clerk's desk. Not to be outdone. He reveals himself to be large and lumbering and at this moment I envy his horns.

He asks the clerk questions he already knows the answers to. "Is my mother awake? Is she ready to go?" He asked these questions only minutes ago.

"No," says the clerk without looking up from her screen. "I'll let you know."

His questions are not addressed to the clerk. But to every one of us in the room. I was here first. I am rhino, the most dangerous animal on the continent.

Perhaps it is the décor. Framed travel posters. Africa. Southern Tibet. Nepal. Urging the waiting family members to dream of far-off places. Or maybe it is just to forget the cold room. And the waiting. We aren't really going anywhere.

"There, there." The middle-aged woman who has been sitting behind me, dressed in an elegant black dress and white overcoat, is quietly zigzagging through the waiting room to the clerk's desk too. I don't see the zebra coming until she has rounded the corner and is suddenly in front of the door.

"Do you know where you are? This is not a war zone." She is so tall and elegant she casts a spell over the room.

"Where are you from? Let me tell about life in Poland. People don't get this kind of medical care. My grandson is in there. Seven years old. We come all this way and waited weeks. Don't be so rude. We are all of us worried."

Taking a position between the two men, she meets them both, eye to eye. Her head is held high, and her ears are tucked back, the way an animal's features react when angered. It will be a mistake if this scene becomes violent. It's clearly not necessary.

But then I can see she is pleading with the men at the counter to back down.

"All right?" she asks. We are meant to be made uncomfortable. Then she trots back to her chair behind me at the far side of the waiting room.

I am speechless. Soon the two men at the counter take a seat. There are flashes of looks between them. She has coaxed them into submission. They will not rise up again until they are called into the recovery room. As each one of the players is called. One after the other. First lion, and then rhino. Then monkey and zebra. Each passes through the door until the room is empty and I am the only one left waiting.

Time slows again. Most of the scenes are running long. The main thread of this spectacle seems to be endurance.

Then suddenly, a woman's voice sounds, like a gun being shot.

Code Blue. First Floor. Northeast corner of the building. Code Blue. First Floor. Northeast corner of the building. She says this over and over. Why does she have to say it so many times?

The woman is not actually in the waiting room. She is backstage and shouting over the hospital loudspeaker. The way a recorded message might say please take your seats; the performance will resume in five minutes. Only her voice is not reassuring.

I am terrified and unsure what to do. It is too late in the performance for this kind of tension. I know what Code Blue means. Somewhere there is a cardiac arrest in progress. It means hurry, resuscitate. Someone might be dying. I am on the first floor. The operating rooms are on the northeast corner of the building. My heart is racing. When elephants die, every one of us comes to the body of the deceased. Where are my people?

I have been here all day separated from my herd. My brain goes white-hot for an instant and then it becomes clear and sharp. Just when I thought the show was coming to an end. Now what? I feel for my tusks. But I have no tusks. I flare out my ears and trumpet a low rumble.

I, the most unlikely theatrical person, am preparing to charge. To climb over the counter. To smash through the door. That door.

I am exploding from the inside out. My heart is screeching like an hourglass drum. Surely the inhabitants in the next village will hear me. You can get through life without having your courage tested. But you can't if you're tuskless.

Then as quickly as my nerves were ignited, they compose. Nothing comes of the code blue in this room. This is all so absurd. The director has entwined the actors and the audience. None of us is a passive observer. Time has moved very slowly and very fast. The show is running overtime. Two hours longer than was scheduled on the program. At last, the door by the clerk's desk opens. The neurosurgeon, now in his street clothes, has come to talk to me. It is only his second appearance of the day. So, the performance begins and ends with the same character. He speaks softly. He isn't trying to impress me. He arrives simply to recap the performance.

"Everything went fine. Superbly. A bull's eye."

While not strictly a play, the show is over. Now we are free to discuss the high points.

"Do you have any questions?" he asks. He has seen this show before and is prepared.

Minutes pass. I want to ask a question, but I can't think of anything. My brain has been in unrest all day, ricocheting between nerves and hope. It has gone on for so long. Not surprisingly, I have become mute by the terrors of my own imagination, and this sudden relief. Before he turns to go, my trunk reaches out, hovers and then presses into his hand, it traces over callouses and bones, furrows and bumps, the ridges of his labour. This reverence. The body speaks everything that matters. Everything that I cannot say. Thank you. Good-bye.

I watch as he leaves. Like a small antelope. Like the wind. He has delivered his skills and is gone. He makes one-legged hops, unaware that anyone is watching. He is on his way home.

So that's how it works. The show lasts all day. No one has invited me backstage. And tomorrow, a stint of warm weather.

You Can't Drive to Kaua'i

I was lying in my bed howling. Wind knocked against the thin pane window of my boarding house room like it was galloping in on a horse in the night. I howled and the wind sang back. I opened my arms and howled again. And once more the wind sang back to me. This day was unique. Like it read my mind. The winds and I became one. Back and forth until the sky grew light and the clouds had vanished.

Vancouver in winter is wet and grey, with an endlessly depressing sameness that dulls everything. Easterly winds don't come through here often, but when they do, they arrive with a holler. A little over ten years ago, a winter easterly ripped through Stanley Park in the middle of the night, taking out power lines, and upturning trees that crushed cars like pop cans. They say that wind uprooted 10,000 trees. I've been waiting a long time for an easterly. I don't want to be angry anymore. The wind grew quiet and so did I. In the lull I whispered, Carry me. Carry me to Kaua'i.

I won't be going to Kaua'i for a beach holiday. I'm going there to start a new life. The sun and those trade winds and the easy life are going to open a new chapter for me. I could feel in my bones the bigness of the adventure I was about to have. This was only my second big risky venture ever. Tanya was the first. I reached across the bed for her. For her muscly, tiny, tough arm.

"I've got the water, two thermoses of coffee and I think I'm going to need twelve Reuben sandwiches from The Bavarian, sweetie. And did you get the Nanaimo bars?"

I could smell the Hawaiian coffee already, and IZ was playing "Somewhere Over the Rainbow" in my head. What I would give to play the ukulele. I began to whistle, picking up my volume above the rattling of the window, trying to wake up Tanya.

"I'm thinking eight days, babe. But I'm planning for twelve. Just to be safe."

I leaned over to kiss her. "I wish you were coming with me." All I held in my hand was a rumpled blanket. Every morning I relived the loss. Tanya was gone. She left me a year ago. And it was my fault.

Once I'd arrived at work at the Granville Island dock and loaded my food and water under the bench of my aquaferry, I put my regrets out of my mind and my mood began to soar. I had to work until 10 p.m. ferrying people from Granville Island to downtown Vancouver and back. Then it would be good-bye city, hello Kauaʻi. November has been a slow month on the aquaferry. There were a few early morning commuters and no one at all taking the aquaferry midday. You'll think I'm crazy, but I rode back and forth on my route, accelerated the engine and screamed, "I love you," into my empty boat.

After that, I got through my day by going over my list and planning my route, waiting for quitting time. Even though my ferry had been empty for the last three crossings, I had to run the route. That's the rule. At exactly 9:55 p.m. just minutes before I was due back at the berth for the night, I pointed my aquaferry west, away from Granville Island. I zipped up my Arc'teryx hoody, wound up the ropes, and ducked my 6'4" body into the pilot's seat. Appearance matters, and I looked smart. I'd bought the jacket with my first paycheque. Cost me the whole wad. A whole week of ferrying locals and tourists back and forth across False Creek. Tanya hit the roof.

"When I said what is the one thing you are going to do today? You know, to be happy. I didn't mean buying a jacket, Chester. I meant little things. Walking in the park. Eating an ice cream cone. Petting a puppy. Jeez, there goes half the month's rent."

The sky was dark but lucky for me a full moon lit the waves of False Creek Inlet and I sailed smoothly under the Burrard Bridge. I loved that bridge. Sometimes I'd get on the speaker and tell my passengers about the history of the bridge. No one ever asked anything, but I liked to point out a few things; the year it was built, the Art Deco style, the number of spans, why it was always being worked on.

Once I made it into the bay, things changed fast. Everything was quiet and the lights of the city were mostly behind me. It was really happening. Just me and my boat and the light we cast a few feet in front of us. I'd overheard one of my earlier passengers say it was going to be a supermoon tonight but in the darkness of English Bay the moon didn't seem so super just yet.

Usually, I would have more than ten people, bicycles, strollers, wheelchairs and dogs in my water taxi, ferrying them across False Creek from Granville Island to Science World, the aquatic center or the casino. I've had cats and parrots and a guy once with a pet iguana. Locals and tourists. It wasn't a walk in the park. It was a lot of work. You got a lot of dumbass questions from people. Like "Where is the exit door?" "Did they barge that casino in?" That's when I'd put my sunglasses on and focus on my job. Weaving in and out between sailboats and kayaks, piloting my passengers safely across the inlet.

I could easily see the lighthouse at Point Atkinson, and I focused on that. The engine hummed quietly and efficiently with an empty load. As long as I stayed in my lane and away from the freighters, I'd be fine. I counted eighteen freighters as I chugged past. All filled to the gunwales with stuff to sell us. Stuff I would no longer need once I got to Kaua'i.

I watched reflections on the water; the condos were lit up on the north side of English Bay. On the south side, the expensive houses had their lights on too. Never been inside one of those. I rolled a cigarette, trying not to focus on the tattoos on my fingers. L-O-V-E and H-A-T-E. Before I met Tanya, I just thought about getting high. Seen lots of my friends go. I didn't expect to have a future.

When Tanya came into my life I was drowning. She was the first person I ever knew worth changing my life for. She had a room then, on East Hastings. She paid the rent until I got a steady job. We lived on food stamps at first, but the room had a good radiator and a month in she got a cat she called Blue that had blue eyes you could see a block away. There was another reason for that cat's name now that I thought about it. At the time I was too blind to see Tanya was smoking pot to get off hard drugs. Or that she was always trying to keep herself from sinking into depression. We were both stuck in our own pain. But she loved me, and I didn't think any woman was going to love me.

A few months after I met Tanya, we moved into a co-op together up on Main. I never went back to my ruined life on Hastings Street. Probably should have married her back then.

The beats of my heart started jumping under my skin. I pulled the lever to speed up my aquaferry. The lights on either side of the inlet started to blur. There was a loudening buzz inside my head. Shit, I hated when this memory came zooming back. It was a year ago and like no time at all. I had come home one day at lunchtime. The ferries weren't running. It was stormy and had started snowing. When I opened the door, I saw Tanya rolling around in bed with some guy with long hippy hair.

I was going to bang the wall with my fist. But I didn't. I walked out the door and down the stairs. Then I turned around and galloped back up. Maybe I had to know who he was. Maybe I had to strangle that guy.

When I opened the door to our room the bed was empty. I called out. No one answered. Not the guy. And not Tanya. Had they slipped out the window? I had auras then and would have premonitions when something bad was going to happen. It sucks being in love.

After that, I walked out into the street shivering wildly from the cold. Snow was falling in little wisps like coming down from heaven. I was dizzy and hungry, and I walked past drunken people. People who were like me. Like I used to be. Stepped over a guy under a blanket covered over by a mangy dog.

When we'd lie in bed talking at night, I used to tell Tanya my dream. That I was going to cruise to Kaua'i.

"Sail, you mean, Chester. In a proper sailboat. Not your aquaferry. Right?"

"No, not my aquaferry. A proper sailboat."

That afternoon I was going to stop and get a bottle of wine.

Get shitfaced. Maybe cop some weed from the dispensary on Main Street. But I went the other way. Turned the corner onto Waterfront Road.

That's when my auras all lined up. Like seeing my dreaming. The way after a crisis happens you can really see where you need to go. Trains arrived. People waved at me, then passed, disappearing into the afternoon light.

There was a sign in a window. Way up high. For Rent. Overlooking Crab Park and the colourful containers stacked up in the port taken off freighters from all over the world. Cruise ships, the heliport and sea buses.

A short lady named Fiona answered my knock. She smelled like cherry perfume.

"Do you have a job, Chester?" she asked after I introduced myself.

"Yes, Fiona, I do. I pilot the aquaferry."

And I had a dream. I didn't say that part to Fiona. I'd started listening to IZ. Israel Ka ano i Kamakawiwo ole. *Somewhere over the Rainbow* was my favourite. And I decided right then, I was really going to do that. I was going to sail to Kaua'i.

I turned on the aquaferry's heater and sank into my seat. The moon was getting bigger and brighter. I had my sleeping bag, pillow and a towel, and the cases of water and the Reubens stowed under the passenger bench. Two cans of gas, planning to gas up at Ganges. Maybe Victoria. These 14-horsepower engines could run forever on a tank of gas. And I had my boom box on, listening to IZ singing "Twinkle Twinkle Little Star" in Hawaiian. I got energy from him that was so pure I couldn't explain it in words. It was a glow inside me. I was starting to miss Tanya.

"Excuse me, *monsieur*. How much longer? What time to arrive?"

Holy shit. Like the wind had smacked me in the face. There was a passenger sitting not ten feet from me in my aquaferry. It was impossible. With that moon casting so much light I made out a man's head with a woolly toque, and a bright orange blanket or skirt or I don't know what. And round dark eyes staring like a ghost. He looked at me; I looked at him. Why hadn't he gotten off? The aquaferry jolted a little and I wasn't sure what to do. All I could hope for was he wouldn't guess we were off-course.

The man spoke again. "We are *en retard*. No?"

I flicked the inside light on. He was a big guy wearing a puffy jacket over a dress. Or maybe an orange robe. And good-looking. He stood up and stuck out his hand at me. "Hello, monsieur. Le bateau, he is late?"

I nodded but couldn't think of anything French to say except *bonjour*. The ceiling of my aquaferry was too low for him. He had to duck his head. The two of us ducked our heads, and then he sat down.

"We're going into the Strait of Georgia. Might be a little choppy but nothing to worry about," I said, as calmly as I could. As though I was the tour guide. I didn't mention the time or docking that wasn't going to happen.

"What hour does he arrive?"

The gusts from the heater caused the hem of his robe to swish from side to side mirroring my pulsing fear. Instead of answering, I waved my hand to quiet him and started asking questions. "Are you French? You sound French. What are you doing on the ferry this late anyway?"

"Oh, please, monsieur, if you could speak more slowly. I have a conférence, and now I go to the Hôtel Sylvia."

"I thought you booked the sightseeing cruise. Ha. Ha." I'm pretty sure he didn't understand a word I'd said.

"I wish to go to my hotel, *monsieur.*"

I turned up the volume on my boom box and the man sat down. He pulled something from his pocket. And lit a match.

"No smoking on the aquaferry," I said, pointing to the No Smoking sign.

The guy had lit a stick of incense and wedged it between the window and the wood frame. He wasn't talking, just sitting and breathing loudly like the wind blowing by.

Right then the ferry started rolling and I quickly grabbed a hold of the wheel and set my sights on where I was going, releasing my thoughts onto the dark churning sea. Under my breath, I cursed the tourist. I wanted to be by myself. This trip was my chance to make a new life. I'd had a miserable year. I'd poured my heart out to Tanya, and what for?

When I moved in with Tanya we lived on the nice part of Main Street. One block from the restaurant Nose to Tail, where she worked as a bartender, with a pig on the window. A fully painted pig. It was a classy joint. They had new postcards every week at the front by the window. You could take one. They were free. I took one every time.

I looked ahead, slowed to veer around a trawler, and was just getting the aquaferry up to cruising speed again when the French guy started talking.

"When is the *terminus*, Chester?"

How did he know my name? I used to turn down my ears when all those crazy people on Hastings Street were yelling at me or asking for money. I had to concentrate now on piloting my boat. Cruising speed could be misleading. It felt slow but there was no question in my mind that I would be travelling past Victoria by morning. Maybe sooner.

"I'm expecting a smooth crossing folks. Well, folk. You. Monk guy. We'll be cruising the Gulf Islands. Galiano and Salt Spring. You could get off in Ganges. A charming small island town with a mountain backdrop. Filled with galleries, restaurants, specialty shops, food and meat markets, even a local post office and bank. I don't know if they have a monastery there but there's lots of people need saving. Have you been to Victoria yet?"

"No, Chester."

I turned around like I was going to drill him. I didn't want to go back to jail. That was a wasted year outta my life. I was angry all the time, pushing people around like they were mincemeat. I didn't have to say anything. He seemed to know what I was thinking. He pointed to my name on the operating licence posted above the door.

"Chester, *c'est vrai?*"

The muscles on the back of my neck were going stiff so I kept talking like it was my job.

"Never been to Victoria? We have to remedy that. You could get off there. Butchart Gardens. Sidney Spit. The Parliament Buildings. Chinatown. Fan Tan Alley. You could have tea at the Empress Hotel. Tourists like that kind of shit." I spit out words like they were stones flying out of my mouth. I didn't care if he understood me or not. I was just trying to put a stop to his questions.

He turned his head and looked out the window without a word. He knew I was angry. I hit the light switch and turned back to piloting my aquaferry. It was maybe an hour later when I turned around again. He was sitting perfectly still and I wondered if he'd fallen asleep. In the dimness, I saw he was still sitting cross-legged. His eyes were open, and he was staring off into the distance like I wasn't even there. I looked him up and down. I doubted he was asleep. He looked like me when I was stoned. The way I would sit perfectly still but my thoughts would be flying. That was an expensive jacket he was wearing. He smelled sweet like I imaged my lei was going to smell when I arrived on the beach in Kaua'i. I got tired of looking and turned back to the water. Soon my eyes drifted shut. I could use a coffee and my stomach was rumbling.

"How about a sandwich? A Reuben with pickle?"

I strained to see if he was done staring. I wanted to say I was sorry for being a jerk. If we're going to be stuck out here together, I imagined we could be friends.

"Come on, caramelized onion and hot mustard on pumpernickel?" There's one thing I learned growing up poor. If you have food, you share.

"No, thank you, *monsieur.* I take a drink."

I sat there in my pilot's seat and I thought I was hearing things. Now the guy was squatting on the bench gazing out the window. He didn't even look at me.

"Water's in the cooler." I came close to yelling "Are your arms painted on?" That would be my old man. Nothing could bring tears to my eyes faster than remembering all the harsh things he used to say to me.

"How many minutes to this Victoria? I like to see her." Then he straightened his legs and got up to get himself a bottle of water.

I turned back to the wheel without saying anything. I was exiting the Burrard Inlet and in front of me was the dark mound of an outline of Vancouver Island. The first night of my adventure I imagined there would be birds or seagulls keeping me company. But there were none here in the open sea. Only the hum of the motor and waves slapping against the bow. And the click of my neck as I glanced back at the monk drinking his water looking smug. I pointed the bow of my aquaferry southwest towards Galiano and Salt Spring Islands and turned my boom box on low and listened to IZ. I wasn't worried about hitting rocks or logs now that we were well past the freighters and out to sea.

I couldn't stay quiet for long. I don't know why because I'm not really all that friendly a guy. It's like I'm making up for all those years I couldn't speak.

"Really? We could catch some fish off Salt Spring Island. Salmon. Lingcod. We could add on a fishing adventure to your tour."

"*Poisson,*" he said. "Fishes?"

"I think so. I mean, I've never fished before. But why not?" There weren't ten feet between us, and I suddenly felt like smiling. Maybe we could be friends.

"Are you angry with me? You know, for taking you with me."

He shook his head back and forth. "*Non, monsieur.*"

"Chester," I said. "You can call me Chester now."

"*Non,* Chester. I am happy."

"Well, monk fella, travelling on the aquaferry can be risky business. You never know who's at the wheel. Or where you're going to end up."

He sat back on his butt, recrossed his legs, straightened his robe, and looked me in the eye. "I don't see everything as rose, Chester."

Even if he wasn't saying much, the truth was I was getting kind of tired of having the monk on my aquaferry.

"I'm going to let you off in Victoria," I said.

After that, he didn't speak, so I didn't speak. Just listened to the sounds of the night; the swoosh of the waves against my boat, the drone of the motor. The sky was brightening already off to the west. It didn't seem like a whole night had passed already. He was breathing in and out loud as a foghorn. And as the light came up, I could see his face looked calm, peaceful. So, I breathed in and out too. Not as loud as the monk's breathing, but like the waves coming in and going out. Smallish waves. If I closed my eyes all I could see was my old man taking a swing at me. He broke my arm three times one year. All in the same place. He was drunk. After that, I never stopped watching. I learned you have to see danger coming and get out of the way.

The monk got up and moved to the open window and practically hung outside. He waved me over. Jesus, there was a pod of Pacific white-sided dolphins swimming along port side. A mass of curved dorsal fins leaped in the air like they were having fun. Even though the window was small, and the monk was tall, and his head was bent at the worst angle, he followed them with his head swinging, up and down like he was the one doing the swimming.

"They follow *poissons*," he said, laughing.

I smiled too, same as him, like I understood why this was a happy thing. And funny thing, I was feeling kind of happy with this damn monk and those dolphins. I turned up IZ and started singing. Like I was swimming myself.

After a while my eyes started to shut, I gestured for him to take the wheel.

"I'm going to get some shut-eye. Driving is easy with a lever to control your speed and a wheel just like a car to steer. Easy peasy. Do you monk guys drive?"

"Yes, *monsieur*. This is no problem."

"We'll head around Sidney Spit. It's kind of early but look out for kayakers. Then I can let you off in Victoria."

I may have fallen asleep. I'm not sure. I knew something was wrong when I looked out over the bow at Harling Point. Jesus, the air was thick with fog and the aquaferry had begun to grunt and groan. The waves were beastly. I took back the wheel. I was a little rough with him but there was no time to explain. I had to get the bow facing into the waves.

"What is this?" he asked in a quiet voice. A whisper. He was pointing to the two towers of the ceremonial altar at the Chinese cemetery, visible through the haze like you could reach out and touch them. The first light of morning was pushing through and the angle of the light set the towers aglow. But distances can be deceiving from the water.

"It's a cemetery for Chinese people. People come to burn joss sticks and offer food. We're not pulling up there," I said. I looked him in the eye. "Just to be clear. Those rocks will split my aquaferry in two like it was a chopstick."

I'd visited the cemetery once with Tanya. What I remembered of Harling Point was the sharp rocky shoreline and how somebody visiting the cemetery said the land was so close to the ocean that winter storms sometimes washed away graves. That seemed excessively negative to me.

Gulls were squawking. The sun was trying to drive out the fog, but it was cold in the aquaferry. I was shivering. What if those graves fall into the sea?

"*Je viens du Viétnam,*" he said, taking out a hanky and wiping his eyes. "They battered us. Beat? Many *morts.* I was *en colère,* Chester. Angry. *Après la guerre, La France,* she gave us a home."

I didn't need to understand every word. I maneuvered my aquaferry in close to the shoreline trying to keep from being tossed by the waves so he could get a look at the cemetery. A strange tremor went through me and shit if tears didn't start running down my face too, warm and stinging.

He pulled off his toque and rubbed the top of his bald head. He was smiling and crying at the same time. I watched closely as he ran his long fingers over his head as though he was uncovering something. His eyes narrowed, and in the curve of his spine, I had not noticed before, he was old.

I didn't say anything, but I kind of loved him then.

"How about a coffee?"

While I steadied the wheel with one hand and poured coffee from the thermos with the other, a gust of wind rocked the boat sending the cases of water to the back of the aquaferry and then to the front. I dropped the thermos and hunkered over the wheel, both eyes on the shoreline.

The thing is, Tanya said she never slept with that hippy guy. She begged me to come back. I couldn't see it. Couldn't make out if she was there or not that day. Was she messing with me? Now she was 4,000 kilometres away in Ottawa living with her sister. I was the one who left her. I walked out of our room in the middle of that snowy November afternoon, just like that. So, I was the one to blame.

My hands were blistering tight on the wheel. I turned up the volume of IZ and started singing. The wind echoed over the sound of my voice. And then a thud. The monk went to the bench and hauled out two life jackets. His boots and the bottom of his robe were swishing in half a foot of water and sandwiches wrapped in brown paper were floating and bobbing. When did that happen?

"We've got to get out of here," I yelled.

He put his hand on my back and handed me a red PFD. I flinched, jumped back. Just about smacked him. It was a reflex. He started screaming. Or was it me who started screaming? I'm not sure.

Tanya never screamed at anything. That's one of the reasons I liked her. I would sit at the bar at Nose to Tail sipping on a cup of tea, and watch her move, mix, shake and pour. I would pull every one of my fingers, cracking my knuckles. Love and Hate. She detested that sound like I was going to splinter my knuckles into pieces, but she'd never yell at me. She'd just roll her eyes.

"*Nous avons frappé un arbre.*"

"A tree? A log." I said. "That's a log. I don't have a cell phone."

"No cell?"

I had flares. Somewhere on the aquaferry there would be flares.

"I can't swim." I screeched. My forehead veins were popping. I could barely hear anything. Or think what to do.

"*Tout le monde nage.*"

"You're talking French. I don't know what you said."

"Swim, Chester."

"I don't know how to swim." My feet flew out from under me and I slid across the wet floor and into a foot of filthy water.

"*Alors, attends!*" He pulled me up, took my hand, and gestured for me to hold the center pole of the aquaferry. Then he wrapped a blanket around me. After that everything went slow. He didn't call me crazy. He wasn't barking orders. Just breathing in and out with a calmness like somebody talking to a friend.

I started speaking. Ranting like I was a tin can pried open.

"I smacked a guy coming out of Blood Alley once. It was a

stupid little thing that got big. Both of us were staring each other down. You learn that living on the street. He snatched my whisky bottle out of my hand. Then I just went off on him. Plowed him in the face. Not a minute later, the cops were cruising the alley, and the dude just went apeshit. The cops called him an ambulance and I got cuffed, thrown into the back of the cruiser, and taken to the clink. Just like that."

"I not afraid, Chester. *Ton ami.*"

Then he pulled a bucket from under the bench and started bailing water from the floor of the aquaferry, which was listing to starboard. Back and forth to the open hatch, he dumped water. Smooth and calm. The bottom of his robe stirred in the slush. Everything was going by me like in a movie.

Out of nowhere, I remembered that I was in charge. I was the pilot. The captain. I had to get us out of this mess. I jumped to my feet and shoved the boat into neutral and dug out the flares. I set one off and then the other. Then I emptied out my sandwich box and started bailing with the box. Son of a gun, the box held the water. When I turned around, I could see the monk in the dimness of the galley sinking his bucket into the water and chucking it out the window. Sinking and chucking. I dipped my box back into the water and got to work.

"Chester, *chantons.*"

Then me and the French guy sang in our loudest voices.

It was noon when a police boat came up beside us. We were red-faced and shivering with gallons of muddy stagnant briny water swishing up to our knees. I was never so happy to see the police in my life. I hugged *Poisson* with all my might. That was when I felt him walk into me. I'll be damned. I laughed, looking down at my ribs, my belly, and around the galley. A door opened and a door closed, and I was alone in my sinking aquaferry. As loud as I could, I breathed in and out, like I was a dolphin rising up out of the sea. It was like a dream when the cop got on the boat, waded through the deep water, to help me onto the police boat.

The aquaferry people let me go. That was a bummer. I'm driving a bus now. Still living in my room at Fiona's on Waterfront Road.

Catching the breezes off the water. I play ukulele on Monday nights with the new bartender from the Nose to Tail.

Tanya sent me a cute card with a picture of a dinghy on the front. "I heard you on the radio, Chester. You really tried to get to Hawai'i. Maybe you should fly next time. xo Tanya."

Well, xo, that means love. I'd send her a postcard, but she never said her address.

So, I sent one to the monk, to Vietnamese French Monastery, Paris, France. I chose one with a drawing of a fish on it. "You are a very big *poisson*," I wrote. "Thank you," I said. "*Ton ami*, Chester." I wrote it like that. With the French words. That'll surprise him.

I need a bigger engine. I think a bigger engine would do it. Fourteen horsepower was too small for the 4,000-kilometre crossing. I'm going to save up and get back in my boat. Because the thing is, you can't drive to Kaua'i.

CHASING RABBITS

When I pulled open the freezer drawer, I was looking for blueberries. What I saw instead was a package of raw bones that looked like tibia or ulna or possibly a femur. They were red and raw, sawed into pieces and frozen in a plastic bag. They were bones for the dogs. But the dogs didn't like these bones. So, I'm going to give them back to the man I purchased them from. With these bones in my freezer I can't sleep at night.

I can't sleep anyway because I'm thinking about you and that girl. That girl was on the news tonight. Some guy in a green bike helmet was on the news too saying how he found her lifeless at the bottom of a slope beneath some leaves when he was out riding his bike. He slid down the path and the girl was lying there like she'd slid too. Only the girl wasn't moving. He uncovered her forehead and her nose and her mouth and he could see she wasn't breathing. How did she get there?

Today was my birthday. Birthdays remind me of coconut cream cakes discovered in summer holiday town bakeries and of chocolate ripple ice cream and long days at the lake in scorching sun.

No, they don't. That's the shred of a memory I cling to like the flapping flag at my childhood summer camp, the canvas faded by wind and weather after summer was gone.

Birthdays stir up a long trail of memories. It doesn't seem to matter how many years, how many birthdays, still the black clouds gather. I was leafing through photographs. Against my will my thoughts started swirling like a twister until they'd picked up everything in my cluttered past and dropped them into the present.

Before I knew it, I was staring at a heap of detritus, trying to make order out of this jumbled life. Maybe I'll never know who's good and who's bad. Who's guilty and who's innocent. No one will help me with this.

It would be easier to walk away and forget everything. Except that my hands are the same as your hands. And I eat my oranges the way you did, cutting them into quarters with the skin on, sucking out the juice like a lemon, until the four emptied-out pieces are all that's left on the plate.

When we were children, you used to walk me home from school. Mom and Dad were never home after school to greet us, so you said, "What's the hurry?" We could walk all over town on the way. We wouldn't get into trouble. Time didn't matter in our family. We would walk down Main Street peering into shop windows until you saw something you wanted to look at and then we had to go inside. You'd sit on the floor at Sorbie's Store reading comic books, gone. I didn't know what to do with myself. I'd walk up and down aisles, look at magazine covers, think about crossing the street to the candy store, but you said, "No, we'll go later." One day I had to pee so badly and you wouldn't help me, so I walked into the alley between Sorbie's store and the Rexall Drugs. No one was there. I backed myself into the wall, closed my eyes and tried to hold on. Then pee dribbled down my leg and over my lace ankle socks and onto my shiny black shoes. I leaned into the wall, not moving, wet and alarmed at what I had done. And finally, when I came to get you, still sitting on the floor reading, you looked up, said nothing and took me home.

Do you remember the summer at the lake you stabbed those Dolly Varden? I didn't even know you owned a knife. You'd caught two or three fish. Maybe more. I figured we would have them for dinner. Dad would have been proud. When it was time to go, you took the fish out of your creel, lay them carefully side by side, on the end of the dock. You forgot I was there. You whispered, "You are beautiful." Then your face grew dark, and you yelled, "You're nothing," and pulled open your sheath and slammed your silver blade, one by one, into their bellies, until the fish stopped wriggling. Hairs crept cold up my neck. A black cloud rolled in over the lake and the air grew icy. I was jittery and chilled and wished for mittens and a wool hat. You never looked up.

I didn't know you then. Not really. Even though we shared the same bungalow, the same parents, most of the same friends, a split-classroom in school. Do you remember the green Peugeot? Our first ten-speed. How I dreamed of that bike after I saw it in the window of the bike shop on Wyandotte Street. I begged Dad, never giving up, until he couldn't be in the same room with me without covering his ears.

"If we're going to buy you two a bike, let's look at the hardware store," he'd said at first. I knew if he could see for himself how elegant and perfect the Peugeot was, all alone on display in the shop window, he'd fall in love with it too.

"Been looking at this bike in the window since it arrived," he said to the salesman, and shook his hand the way he shook everyone's hand down at *The Observer*. "Editor of the paper," he said. He was proud of that. "Now here's a bike I would have loved when I was young." A real air of confidence. Acting like the whole thing was his idea. Which was weird because what he said to us was that bike was a racing bike and not a bike for a couple of kids. The salesman described all the fancy racing features: the steel construction, Japanese gears, French Reynolds tubing. What was a *derailleur*? I didn't dare to ask. He did it naturally, not pushing the sale. Then he saw the light in my eyes, looked at me and said, "Can't think of a nicer way to get to school than on this baby."

I still can't believe Dad bought the Peugeot. He was such a tight wad. But he did buy it. And we had a kind of freedom with that bike, didn't we? For a few months. Then you stopped bringing it home. "It's at Mitch's place. Go get it if you want it," you said when I pestered you. Your eyes never leaving the television. I'd go after it for a while. Then I got fed up and asked Dad to make you bring it home. You never did. One day Mr. Bradley, our math teacher, brought it back to our place. Said he found it on his front lawn and recognized it right away. The chain was rusted, the gears were locked up and I was shocked at how old and creaky it was after such a brief time. The paint was chipped, and I could barely make out the block lettering that spelled PEUGEOT on the tube.

My eyes got watery. I knew no one in our family was going to repair that thing. I never rode our bike again.

Where did you go? Once or twice, in my dreams, I found my old walking shoes and met you on the road. I'd be on the path we used to take, out of town, over the Maitland River, where we'd climb up the east bank, then walk along the CPR tracks, listening for the train. I loved our walks. Going nowhere. "See where the nose takes us," you'd say. Mostly we were silent together. Once I asked you about what she'd done. I'd heard you crying in your room. You plucked a leaf from a hanging branch. "I don't care," you said, nonchalant. It was the only time you spoke of her. I never forgave her. She's an old woman now, the one who pointed your nose into a filthy brown carpet and kicked you with her heavy brogues.

You were braver than me; you walked all alone into the cemetery and ate your lunch among ancient red oaks and our French-Canadian Scottish ancestors, and yelled back at me, "Come in, there are children in here." I never did. I said I was afraid we'd get caught. I was actually afraid of the small headstones with angel wings. Then you met me back on the trail, clicked open your pocketknife, aimed it at a tree, flung it until it stuck, and we were wild with laughter.

The last time I visited our mother I stole a handful of photos. When she wasn't in the room, I stuck them in my coat pocket. There was one grainy black and white photograph of you and me. We were five or six then, crammed around a picnic table in party clothes and paper hats, with a bunch of our friends I don't even recognize anymore. We were young children with fathers and mothers. The picnic table was set with wildflowers and paprika eggs, fresh peaches, and lemonade. And birthday cake, of course.

Today is Nelson Mandela's birthday too. He would have been ninety-nine years old today. He was eighty-seven when he published his autobiography. You mailed his book to me one summer for my birthday. No return address. Not even a note. How long are you going to go on like this? I read once that when the wheels come off a chariot, they don't all come off at once. They fall off one at a time; until one day the chariot is parked and abandoned on a rutted road and it doesn't run anymore.

I read the book, all 630 pages, the day it arrived. I sat out in the backyard until the sun was overhead and my eyes were seeing dots instead of words. Then I moved inside, poured a bowl of blueberries, and flattened myself out on the couch until I was halfway through. By noon the dogs managed to position themselves, one at my feet and the other one at my arm, desperate to go out, so I took a break, and walked them to Spanish Banks. They rolled in the mud at low tide. I walked barefoot, the thick mud oozing between my toes like frothy pumice, further and further, towards the sea.

The Good-bye Graffiti guy was at the beach again, rolling paint with a giant roller over the retaining wall. One day graffiti. The next day paint over. Back and forth. I wanted to read the whole thing from the very beginning. All the words written under that putty-coloured paint. Somebody was trying to say something. The Good-bye Graffiti guy drove off. I laughed at myself staring at a blank wall, leashed up the dogs, rinsed my feet and we climbed the hill back home.

After that, I spread my yoga mat on the ground, lay down and read until I'd finished the whole thing. Mandela's eighteen-year imprisonment on Robben Island, his lifelong struggle against apartheid in South Africa and his life after his release when he became president of the African National Congress. That's a lot of life for one man. There are parts of his story I never knew. His given name was Rolihlahla. It means to pull a branch from a tree.

If you want to understand forgiveness you should have a dog. Once I was so angry with you for hanging up the phone on me, I threw my coffee cup across the room. It landed on the floor and shattered like mirror glass. I cried and pushed one of the dogs out of the way when he raced to me. Still he licked my face and sat by me. A dog will offer forgiveness, not once or twice, but endlessly. Like it says in the Bible, seventy times seven. My two terriers come from the West Highlands of Scotland. They are tough and stubborn, their temperaments forged from the harsh northern weather and geography, like ours are supposed to be.

But they are hunters too. In the eastern corner of Jericho Park, where we walk every day, there is a rabbit warren. I was shocked at how crazed the dogs became the first spring day we walked there. I wasn't thinking and had both dogs off-leash. The rains had stopped and the smell of the earth and the sea and first blooms of crocuses were in the air. The kind of afternoon you want to bookmark. Then their stubby noses rose up. I forget they have an olfactory bulb forty times the size of ours. When they smell something, they don't ignore it. They took off, effortlessly sliding under thorny brambles I had to shoulder my way through. Branches and more branches until I was inside. Then it was like a door had closed. Suddenly we were in another world of circular paths worn like a racetrack and smaller paths and blocked paths and dirt piled into heaps that hid the holes to the entrance of burrows and underground tunnels. I could see nothing but the hind end of them as they spun around out of sight. They raced through the warren with me chasing after them half mad with fright. Finally, they positioned themselves, motionless, at the opening of a burrow, waiting. It was raining again by then and they were soaked and shivering and the daylight was ending. Their focus unnerved me. If a rabbit had come out of that hole, it was not going to go free. And who would be to blame?

Why did you send me that book?

I want to ram somebody with the heel of my boot. I've wanted to do that for a long time. The problem is I don't know who to ram. I am glued to my seat at the dining room table and watching as she yells at you. "Where were you? All I asked you to do was to mow the lawn. Can't you do anything you're asked? Come and go as you please. What do you think I'm running here? A boarding house?" I'm shaking so hard I spill my milk. Then she yells at me too. But it's you who had to go sit in the cellar until dinner was over. If Mother were here now, I'd lock her in the coat cupboard. I've been alone in that cupboard a long time waiting for her. It's quiet in the cupboard. The cupboard is like a mudroom, the anteroom between the outdoors and the house. There are coats and winter boots. Crates stacked in the corner with vegetables. And boxes of the old speeches she wrote for the mayor. Taped and marked with the year. All her life an assistant. Never the mayor. The cupboard is cold.

After the news story with the guy in the green bike helmet I turned off the TV and went out into the yard and gazed up at the sky. I saw only crows. Then an eagle flew overhead. I was looking for you in the cumulus clouds. At first, I couldn't see anything, just white shapes like inkblots in the dimming sky. Then I saw your nose, your chin—saw you—the way you would run, with one arm swinging out from your side, like a busted wing. Remember when your friend Gael asked, "What are you running from?" I wanted to flatten her then. "I'm just running," you said.

I saw you only once since you left home. Ten years ago, at Granville Island Market. You were shockingly thin, sinewy as a tightrope walker, your pants hitched high and belted at the waist. I began walking towards you when I saw there was a young girl beside you tugging at her too-snug dress. Well, that was our minister's daughter. As soon as I recognized her, I froze. I couldn't take my eyes off her. You swatted her hand until she stopped, lowered her eyes, and gripped the strap of her purse. The girl was wearing red lipstick. She was uneasy and too young for those things. What was that girl doing there with you? I'm ashamed now that I didn't say something before you disappeared into the crowd. I wanted to call out to you, "Come back. We'll do this over." What I should have done was call out to the girl. "Look out!"

I walked backwards, turned and hurriedly crossed Granville Island, past stalls of fruits and vegetables, the woodworking co-op, fishing boats, and through Vanier Park. The wind pushed against me. I pushed back for over an hour without stopping. You had kin. That knowledge burned into my brain with every step. I walked further and further from you.

As soon as I reached my little house with the two white dogs and the stacks of books and cupboards that are full, I sat on the floor. And when I couldn't wait any longer, I picked up the phone and called Mother.

When she said hello, I started to cry. Sun burned into the room and there were dust motes and the room was a river and I was floating and bobbing, and the river was all current and shallows and bends and falling rock.

I asked if she'd talked to you lately. "Your brother was unlucky all of his life. Nothing worked out for him," she said. "I don't believe it was his fault." I'm trying to hug her. I'm hugging a slippery hollow of driftwood with stories and no podium. Assistant to the mayor but never the mayor. I should have asked about the girl. I should have phoned someone else. Someone who would have protected that girl.

I crawled over the carpet. Across continents and into darkness. I crawled back onto the couch. "Stop varnishing," I said to her. "Do you hear me?" But I had hung up the phone already.

I live by a school. I see you in every child who walks by. Then I closed my eyes and I imagined that girl. Only now she is no longer a child. No one was speaking. I pulled the scene back like I'm a wide-angle lens trying to see the whole room. I'm searching for a window. Or a door. An entry place where the rescuers might have broken in to save her. The body was quiet. Her wrists were red and bent like wire hangers. I hate that my imagining takes me back to you.

I can't sleep. I toss and turn in my bed. There is pressure on my head. I push back on it with the palm of my hand. The pressure doesn't stop. I heard voices passing in the street. Men's voices. One sounds like a radio announcer. I remember our mother and father sitting in the living room talking in low voices. I am at the top of the stairs listening. I am wearing pajamas. The room is dark, save for the red light of Father's cigarette. The red light is dancing. They are mumbling. I move down a step. Then two more steps. Straining to hear. "We will… He has to go. There are hospitals." "No. What are you talking about?" I listen, stretching my ears down the staircase. I know something is wrong. "We have to send him somewhere," she says. "No," he says. Secrets whispered in darkness. He taps his cigarette into an ashtray. The room is dark again.

If I call the police this will be in the newspaper. Dad's newspaper. People will know. The dogs are restless and don't settle until I lift them onto the bed. There is a moment in the chase when the rabbit stops running and sits still. Does it stop because it has given up or because it will blend in with its surroundings and all eyes will be diverted for the time being? At that moment it will retreat to its hole and safety. I always forget they have done this before.

No one in our family is going to repair this thing. It's the middle of the night. I don't even know where you are. God forgive me. Before morning. Before light washes in.

The Same River Twice

"No man ever steps in the same river twice, for it's not the same river and he's not the same man." —Heraclitus

On the morning of my thirtieth birthday, I woke with a splinter throbbing under my thumbnail. I had been dreaming that I was getting married. But I am not getting married. My sister is getting married. I am getting divorced. I lay in my bed in no hurry to begin my day, watching two crows on a branch outside my window and intermittently digging at the splinter with the end of a pin that was there on the night table. The crows caught my attention because they were leaning into each other, unmoving, as if they were a mated pair. People say crows are simple, but they are not simple. They also, I've read, mate for life. I, on the other hand, was turning thirty, waking up alone in a king-size bed, having just discovered that my husband slept with my best friend.

My driver's licence was about to expire, so I forced myself out of bed, pulled on a sweater and drove to the Motor Vehicle Branch. I handed over my old licence to a clerk with a tattoo that said *Awake to Love* on her neck. That must have been painful. She was humming as she took my information. I was standing on giant footprints to have my photo taken, afraid I was going to burst into tears, when I heard a bell go off. The kind of ringing clapper that sounds in the night, when you are all alone, chiming out truths. Stop being a marshmallow. I looked up at the clerk and blurted a wrong address. I don't know why I did this. I am generally an honest person. The next morning the clapper sounded again. Change your name.

I've always liked the name *Aila*. It means "from a strong place."
That's a little far-fetched but I have hopes just the same. What of
that saying, "look where you want to go, not where you've been."

In February, the month before my birthday, I'd flown back to
Halifax to visit my ailing aunt. When I returned home to Vancouver, my husband David was unusually quiet. The house was newly
cleaned and he was lying on the bed watching a hockey game.
There was an empty bottle of Pinot Noir in the recycling bin and
a broken wine glass. I was certain I smelled cigarette smoke too.
Then I went around the house looking at everything. Digging in
the garbage, at scraps of paper on the desk by the telephone, in the
pocket of his jeans in the laundry bin. Every so often he looked
up at me from the hockey game. Not saying anything. Partly by
chance, I opened the door to the hot tub. My wet bathing suit
was hanging on a knob, smelling of chlorine. There was a moment
of silent nothing, and then I just floated out of my life. Inside
my head, I was ticking and whirring blackness. Like in a fugue. I
was flying over the bedroom. I was about to interrupt the hockey
game. Somewhere, already grieving the things disappeared.

I could have joined a group with other people who had been
cheated on. In a stranger's garden over white wine and canapés,
I could have cried. Someone would have held my hand, said, "I
know how you feel" as I rewound the past, forming better sentences, new and improved reasons why my husband had an affair
with my best friend. My story would have garnered the most sym-
pathy.

But I went my own way. Instead, I bought a rebuilt Vitus,
a classic French racing bike and now I cycle everywhere. I train
every day, after work, on weekends, in all weather. I've learned
French names: *cycliste, vélo, derailleur, cadence*, and *peloton*. I've disappeared into this new language. It has given birth to something
different in me I didn't know I had. I've become strong and fast,
and fixed in my new pursuit.

During the past few months I ran into David once or twice.
The first time, I was shocked at how much weight he gained, and
his blond thatch of hair was uncharacteristically unruly, giving him
a wild look. One day he was leaving Liberty Wines as I was on

my way in and passing each other was unavoidable in the narrow entry. I wasn't ready for feeling sorry for him. He looked like a man dragging around half the continent. "I miss you, Lisa," he said. He leaned in like he was going to touch me but didn't. He had one hand wrapped around the neck of a bottle of something called Nota Bene. His voice was crackly and high, and I couldn't help noticing how he was clutching his car keys in the other hand, rubbing them like he'd expected a genie to appear. He wrote his cell number on the back of his receipt and handed it to me. "Call me?" he asked, with that voice again. Then someone heading into the store knocked into me and our time was up.

He hadn't denied the affair. But he wouldn't talk about it either. "We've had five great years; please don't end it over one stupid mistake." At the time he was vacuuming, squeezing the canister between the dining room chairs. He hardly looked at me. That's all he said. His only reference to sleeping with my best friend.

Then in August, six months after I'd changed my address and was calling myself Aila, a curious thing happened. I was on a blind date with a man at a farm dinner. I had been reluctant about the set-up and feeling awkward in a group of strangers when I was handed a glass of sparkling wine and herded onto a pathway by a chatty woman who had the black hair and girlish face of Björk. Her name tag said Lone Star. There were about sixty of us who had paid two hundred dollars a ticket to gather in an unmowed field, surrounded by rows of barely sprouting lettuces, spinach, arugula and kale, to listen to a lecture about crop rotation, sustainability, becoming locavore, how everything we eat can be grown in our own backyards. She was pitching how we could become a friend of the farm when I spotted David.

He wandered over and didn't stop approaching until he was touching me. He smelled good. Familiar. "Nice bracelet," he said, eyeing the crocheted silver cuff dotted with tiny blue sapphires on my wrist. He gave me that bracelet for my birthday two years ago. My hand went to the bracelet, slowly twirling it around. It was like when someone says, Don't think about a pink elephant, and then that's all you can think about. My brain went empty except for the bracelet, my ex-husband and that birthday.

"You alone?"

"No."

"Me neither," he said. "Well, nice to see you, Lisa."

Then Lone Star said it was time to begin our tour of the fields, the children's garden, the garden given to the ten lucky interns, farmers in training, the First Nation's garden, and wasn't there some guy off by the trees with a shopping buggy, looking over at us and pissing on the plot.

"Let's go, Aila," said my date.

"Aila?" asked David.

"I'm just trying it out," I said, brushing him off. He was thinner and handsomer. "We should get moving. I'm getting bitten," I said, shooing away mosquitos. David put his fingers on my arm. Lightly, like a bird landing. He leaned in close and in the littlest whisper, like raindrops, I think he said, "I want you."

"Well, nice to see you," he said, in his bright regular voice.

Then he sped up to join his date for the walk about the farm. I begged myself not to look, but that was near impossible; she was wearing a skirt with red polka dots and black sunglasses like Jackie Onassis. She was beautiful. I never pictured him with a blond. She was leading the pack, teetering precariously along the rough dirt path in cork wedges. And I thought, son of a bitch, he landed like a champ.

The group of us trampled across the wet bumpy earth, where a tractor had made the road rutted. It had been raining all day and the ground was hard and slippery at the same time, and walking was awkward, though I was gripping the ground just fine in my sandals with thick rubber treads and my new strong cycling calves. The sun broke through the cloud cover and began releasing the scent of nettles, honeysuckle and lavender. The smell of sweetness made me ache for the sumptuous garden David had made in our backyard, overgrown and in need of pruning now. We walked first through the children's garden where there was a wall of sweet peas against a trellis. I stopped to take a photograph.

"This isn't the garden. The actual garden starts over there," my date said, grabbing a hold of my arm and pointing to a long, rowed field below where we were standing. My eyes followed his hand across to the ploughed fields and back to the wet grass and the first sunlight of the day pouring onto the string of sweet peas. A minute ago they had looked wilted and finished, now they were peeling back and reaching towards the light. I didn't say anything, kept taking my photograph.

As we exited the garden, a wiry guy wearing a red kerchief around his head directed us to sit at the table. One of his arms was completely tattooed in tiny pitchforks. He instructed us to choose a plate from a mismatched pile on a wagon. By the time we were seated at the long row of joined tables in ankle-high grass, I'd already finished off that glass of sparkling wine and two glasses of Pinot Gris, feeling woozy and ready to go home. As I took my seat I was thinking, *not every story has a happy ending.*

The dinner was a lot of courses with cured meats and pickled vegetables served in mason jars and almost none of the scant greens we had viewed earlier in the garden. At first people had their iPhones out taking photos of the food, but then they stopped and you could feel the excitement waning. There was almost nothing on the table worth getting excited over.

Rain kept threatening throughout the meal. Intermittently, streaks of sunshine broke through, which made the sky both ominous and intriguing. I was seated at one end of the table and David was way down past the middle where I couldn't see him or the polka dots. Lone Star walked the length of the table, explaining each of the courses, "The peas and the pea shoots were picked just an hour ago." I wondered from where. Three young women beside us, twenty-something foodies, were funny and charming like bees buzzing at our end of the table. Before the first course arrived, they'd provided a lively discussion about corn sex. Who knew corn was such a difficult vegetable to fertilize?

I could see my date eyeing the see-through sparkly blouse of the woman seated on the other side of him and by his third or fourth glass of Merlot he started saying how eight courses was too many and two hundred dollars a ticket was morally wrong. "You could feed all of the homeless people on Hastings Street for that." By then we'd all had too much to drink and no one wanted to be reminded of homeless people.

The sun had long ago dropped below the tree line and our chattering group grew silent. We exchanged phone numbers and the young women at the end of the table called a cab and tottered off like crabs into the night. I was halfway to the parking lot when I felt for my bracelet and noticed it was gone. I rooted through my open purse and into the creases of my scarf. "I'll meet you back at the car," I said to my date following the grassy path back towards the table. Light was fading, I could tell he wasn't listening. He was scurrying to catch up to the woman who had sat next to him. There I was, suddenly all alone, under the blue-black sky. I wasn't hopeful of finding such an intricate piece of jewelry. The grassy area seemed larger now with the people gone.

I was about to give up looking but felt compelled to get down on my knees and at least cover the area around my chair. It was cold and I was fuzzy-headed from all the wine, and the mosquitos were biting again. Then I got into a kind of tempo, like on a long bike ride when the pacing comes and the tiredness turns into a second wind and you find a strength you didn't know you had. I ran my fingers through the thick dewy grass, determined that somewhere, in this unruly meadow was the thing I was looking for.

There was a faint voice above my head. "Didn't you get enough to eat?"

"What are you doing here? Where's your date?" I asked.

"She left with the guy seated on the other side of her."

"I'm sorry," I said.

I looked at his face, waiting for my eyes to adjust to the near dark. David looked older, but content. Calmer. The same and not the same. Incredibly attractive.

"I lost my bracelet."

We crossed and re-crossed the damp field on our hands and knees, with me following behind, trying to chase a whiff of him. I had an absurd urge to lift my leg and pee on the path he'd flattened. The sky was dark, I felt raindrops and finding my bracelet was becoming hopeless. But I was feeling surprisingly strong from all that cycling, flushed by the wine, and the clapper was striking again, trilling inside my skull. I began crawling like I was driving a tractor. Like we were chasing each other into the coming night. Incapable of giving up.

"Are you really changing your name?" David called out.

Before I could answer, he shouted, "I've got it," plucking the bracelet out of the folds of grass like it had suddenly broken free. He found my hand and slid the cuff onto my wrist.

"Happy birthday, Aila," he said.

Without pause we propped each other up until we were standing. The ringing in my head had gone quiet and I could think of nothing to say. The wind was up, and above us a steady flapping and cawing of crows traversing the field. Incredibly loud. Coming together and moving apart as the dark settled. We stood motionless in the moonlight, watching the sapphires blinking, like children seeing fireflies for the first time.

INTERDIT, PARIS

In the photograph on the back of my copy of *The Vagabond* there was a vase of orange roses on Colette's tomb. This was surely wrong. White roses, I was told by my friend René, were her favourite. I trusted René. He was worldly and has been everywhere. This was my first trip abroad. We were both studying French literature at the Sorbonne in Paris, where we would live for the next six months. And we were both reading Colette's book. That's how it all began.

I noticed him with his book the day I arrived. I was registering and waiting for my room key and clutching my copy like a string of worry beads. René was perched in a corner of the university foyer sketching on the cover of his copy and every so often he'd look up at me and smile. Causing a huge wave of excitement to wash over me. *Confrère.* I was standing on the edge of something. And him there, shimmering. Out of the corner of my eye, I saw his rosy cheeks and black jacket. And a black knit cap pulled low as if trying to contain his wild blond hair. Already hip. Though it was September and not actually cold yet in Paris. Then I noticed he had earbuds in and possibly wasn't even looking at me at all and I felt awkward.

At that moment he caught my eye. "That's a good book," he yelled across the hall.

"Which class are you in?"

"Section A for the fall term."

"Me too." He had a sultry voice, deep and rich and I could imagine him reading his work aloud, like a jazz player, holding onto every beat. I followed a slanting ray of light as he got to his feet and crossed the lobby. There was nobody else but me left in the foyer. He pulled out his earbuds, reached his hand out, and I could barely speak. Saturday morning on my first day in Paris and I already had a friend. What more could I want?

"Hey, I should get your number. I've been here for a month. It's no fun hanging out in Paris alone."

He uncapped his pen and made a line drawing of a bird on the cover of his copy and wrote my cell number on the open wing. I could never write on the cover of a book. But as I stared at his drawing that day, I was beginning to learn, there will be nobody like René. He makes his own rules.

Later he would say that it was my spiky hair with the purple streaks that reminded him of his favourite grebes in the city park at home. Something funny and familiar that got him talking to me. Although he has a French name, René's from Oslo. Not French at all. I am Ayleigh Stewart, pronounced *Ay-lee*, not *Ay-la*. When I arrived, other students guessed from my name that I was Scottish. I'm not. I'm Canadian. I'm also a little French. I've kept this to myself. Though I liked to believe it means something. That like Colette, I'll arrive. Find her smartness and daring. Her lipstick and pantaloons. Her reveries. That I would write like her and one day press my own book in my hand.

I soon learned that René wrote poems. He could recite poetry by heart. The weather had been good for autumn and after class we had been cycling alongside the river to the Café des Artistes, sharing *un pichet* of wine, and reading to each other. The drinking age here is eighteen, so I felt very chic sipping red wine for the first time. René swore there is no drinking age in Norway, which I found hard to believe. He was always drawing. His journal was filled with words but also birds, wolves and horses. Right from the beginning there were no silences between us. It was like we had known each other forever. He read as we sipped our wine. He'd take a deep breath, fumble with his journal, search the dog-eared pages, and then begin. His poems seemed to have no reservations. Every chip on his shoulder was unlocked and exposed with a fury as he read. When it was my turn to read, I'd choose carefully, reading from the beginning of my notebook. Words I'd written before I started down the dangerous path of asking questions. Before I began to push against the secrets in my own family.

"Jesus," he said. "Your poems are whisperings. Where would we be if the greats wrote like that? You ought to let go."

"We are not all screamers," I said, annoyed. "Anyway, I have others."

We talked of Colette too. I have *un petit peu* of her free spirit. But I'm not the rogue she was. I glanced at my bike resting against a tree, glad that I'd made the effort to box it up and cart it all this way. It was getting late and with my arms bare I had begun to shiver with the cold. I pulled my scarf tighter. "Did you know she worked in the circus and the dance halls of the Moulin Rouge?" I said. "She had marriages and affairs. And lovers; gay and straight." I said this a bit too fast. Proud of everything I knew, I emptied myself out. Waiting for his reaction.

"I didn't know that. Cool."

"And dig this, she had an affair with her step-son. I could never do that. Any of it."

"I bet you could," he said, smirking at me from across the table.

"I can't imagine." I fidgeted with my paperback on the table-top, turning it to the back cover. "I don't mean that I want to. But, you know, for a woman, there are so many rules." We were both staring at the photograph of her tomb. "In the end she was given a state funeral, the first woman in France. They didn't punish her."

"I've seen her tomb," he said. "She was buried in Père Lachaise Cemetery with all of the most esteemed Parisians."

"Really? As though she had been loved all along."

"Why do you think she wasn't?"

I looked at him with astonishment. Emptied my glass and felt just the littlest bit intoxicated. "She was outrageous."

"I'm just telling you the facts, Ayleigh. Have you been?"

"To the cemetery? No." By now my head was swimming with the wine, or the wine and the possibilities. Everything was so new. "I want to go," I said. "Let's go."

René leaned back in his chair and smiled. Shook his head no.

"Ah, come on," I begged. But he refused.

"I went there already. In August when I arrived in Paris. This is your thing now. Go see for yourself. I hope you find something." What did he mean by that? I didn't ask. It was quarter to six. The café was setting up for dinner. It was time for us to pay for our drinks and head back to our *résidence*. We collected our bikes and cycled across the square and out to the street.

That night, I lay in my bed unable to sleep. I opened the window and stared out into the Paris night. The light, traffic, and voices of the Latin Quarter never growing dim entered my thoughts like shadows. I'd come all this way. I didn't want to be cowardly now. By morning I had hatched a plan.

On the following Friday I set out after class. I stopped first at the Marché aux Fleurs. A dozen white roses, I requested. Wrap them in pink parchment. I tied the package to the back of my bicycle. I had brought brandy too. Expensive and French. "You have to court a lady," René had said. "It'll get her talking."

It was five o'clock and the light was still like summer when I was finally inside. The gates would close at 6 p.m. The weight of my pack with the flowers, brandy, *The Vagabond*, my headlamp, and my notebook with my own poems strapped onto my back.

I saw to my surprise that Père Lachaise was like a village. One hundred acres of trees and hilly cobblestone streets. I walked and walked, looking for her grave. René said buy a map, but I didn't want to be seen by anyone. There was Rossini. And Jim Morrison, of course. Oscar Wilde's tomb was encased in plastic and covered with lipstick kisses. There was no one here to ask why. Frédéric Chopin. Édith Piaf. Marcel Proust. I walked further and further into the quiet peacefulness of the walled garden. Unsure of where I was going. Each tomb unique, ornate, and above ground. Some of them were grotesque. Chestnut trees were in full sparkling leaf of early autumn and black birds cawed, screeching like old violins. There was an elderly couple ahead of me, walking hand in hand. How does love find itself among the dead? I had locked my bicycle a few feet from the entrance gate, guessing I would be in here for an hour. Maybe two. But the sun was moving low under the full trees. There was so much to see, I was soon unaware of the time passing.

The bells of nearby Notre-Dame began to ring. Despite hearing them every morning and evening since I'd arrived, they caught me off guard. So enchanting. I was an ordinary person who had never travelled beyond my own small town and suddenly I was in the most fascinating city in the world. A cascade of sound washed over the tombs and then the sound ceased. I'd read that the bells of the church were silent for four years during WWII when the city was occupied.

The gates of Père Lachaise would be locked. I was an intruder now. My eyes fell to the crooked cobblestones. There was a black cat meandering at my side. Then I noticed there was a rush of cats behind me. Were they stalking me? I walked a little faster, glancing at the names on the tombs, but not stopping. It was not that the many tombs were uninteresting to me. But I was alone, the cemetery was massive, and I had to keep a pace. Further along, the street curved in on itself like a labyrinth. The tombs became grander in the near dark. I passed by busts of the dead, grey gargoyles, life-size angels weeping, ornate doors on mausoleums the size of small houses. There was a wall dedicated to the Jews and resistance fighters of World War II. It was impossible not to feel nervous being alone and a little overwhelmed surrounded by the most important French people who ever lived. The small gifts I brought with me seemed nothing in the midst of this history and grandeur.

What was I doing here among these dead bodies? I thought I heard voices. And became convinced I could hear breathing. René hadn't said these streets would go on forever. Just as I was cursing myself for not buying the map, I saw *Ici Repose Colette.* 1873–1954. That was all. Unadorned. No flowers. I walked across the grass to lay the white roses I'd bought on the flat surface of the tomb. And then the bottle of brandy. The leaves of the trees were fluttering. I was shaking. I scrambled up the ledge and sat on the raised tomb. There were shadows and quiet and trees that made a dark forest around her. I thought of home and why I had come to Paris. All my dreams swirled inside me like an eddy. Were there spirits here in Père Lachaise? I sat and waited. Would I talk to her? And in what language? I slid my fingers over her name. The light grew dim. I noticed after a while that my head was bowed. I must have dozed.

"*Poète?* Well, *Madame.* Read something."

I startled. What was that? A vague pearly figure was sitting on the end of Colette's tomb. A small woman. Even in the fading light, the image was unavoidable. My nose filled with scents. Earthy and sweet. My chest hammered. I was bursting. Was she greeting me? I shook with goosebumps but was strangely clear headed.

"I am to read something?" I asked. I sounded formal and urgent.

"How is your voice? One must have a very high voice when reading."

We were having a conversation. Colette and me. Under a spreading chestnut tree in Père Lachaise Cemetery. The dimming light glimmered on the white rose petals. This was all so mysterious and unexpected. I opened my notebook and began.

When you come, we could walk
around the pond,
spring is early this year,
I expect the maples and aspens are
already in bud,
How they will please you, when you come.

"That is *très jolie.* But what is it about?"

"Love," I say.

"*Oui,* but love is risky and *extroaordinaire. Non?* Are you speaking to a lover? Then you must be *un peu risqué. N'est-ce pas?* Love is not safe and ordinary. In love you swing from the highest rafters. There is no net."

Was I peeking in through a window? René said Colette worked from her bedroom. One floor up. Writing on a small legless table on the daybed. But on the garden level was the theatre. Everything was hush. This was strangely like a heavy curtain had parted. She was swinging from a trapeze. In a pink chiffon *pantalon.* So little light to make out where she was. But no one else had the face of Colette. The perfect French nose. The warmly lit hair piled high on top of her head, spilling down her neck like a mane. Darting back and forth from one end of the room to the other, like a bird. Flitting. Yes, flitting.

"I learned to be a successful performer. When I was fourteen, I met a boy who changed my life. Read some more," she said from her trapeze. She had no harness.

I will watch down the path for you,
follow the sun rising
to the east,
although I do not see it from the house
it will come.

When you come, we will make plans.
So much ahead of us still.

"You are not taking enough risk. You are going to die. I tell you this because of the war. We did not know what was around the next corner. Poetry is best suited to difficult times. Its function is different. Direct, emotional, patriotic." Her hands were stretched outward, her legs bent. She hurled herself off the platform again. She was flying.

Who was I to be reading to Colette?

"The medium is dead now. *Complètement mort.* Take up painting. Everyone is fawning over the Impressionists. Even Picasso, after the liberation of Paris, he paints light. The war tortured him. Do you know Guernica? It will be this century's most famous anti-war painting. I am sure of it. With art, it is difficult to get the balance right. It comes to you in the street. In the dark. The events of your life are a branch. The artist is a bird looking for its own branch."

All of this she managed while swishing back onto the platform, clutching the trapeze.

"It's a story in a way," I say. I was standing. Ready to prove something. "The lovers meet." I pushed on.

Later on,
we sit in the yard, in the warm sun
of mid-day,
I feed you, and we laugh
our bellies full.

"Yes, but think of the great stories. Sartre's *L'Etre et le néant* and *Les Mouches*, and Camus' *L'Etranger* and *Le Mythe de Sisyphe*. The stories ache. A story can be anything. But you must not seek anyone's approval."

I returned to my notebook. I read more.

When you come you will rest your head,
such a long journey
so much to speak of
When you come.

"We were all happy to be alive too. Especially after the war. But it did not come so easily. Parisians did not go to sleep one night and wake to the bells of the churches. To the liberators arriving. There was struggle and pain. Much sadness. Loss. You see?"

My poem was a flop. I saw this now. Surprised by how chastised I felt. I was surrounded by the dead and uneasy about all this talk of the war. I caught my breath. And tried to begin again. Almost choking on my words.

Then, like a shooting pain, revealing so clearly things that had been waiting, there was my grandfather, Christopher. So real in this moment. The year was 1944. He was in Lille, in the north. I was watching him, alone and walking to the home of his girlfriend, the young French girl, Mathilde. I have stumbled over a threshold. I knew he would survive the war and they will marry. They will take a boat to Canada, have children, one will be my father. I walked beside him, trying to look into his eyes, but they were glazed over, he did not see me. Both he and Mathilde will die before I am born. France and the war will never be spoken of in my family again.

"What do you see?" she whispered. I tried to push away my vision. Memory was suffering.

"Before," she says. As though she knew my banished tears wait to be liberated.

Does he know he has survived the war? He has been three years in the trenches. Cold and muddy, unrelenting rain, wet and hopeless. There was little colour, everything pale and faded. But memory once delivered cannot be forgotten. The rusty smell of trucks and tanks, stagnant water and unwashed men penetrated the still night. Bloated bodies and decomposing flesh. Smells so unpleasant, that once they came to me, they took over and couldn't be undone. She had a point.

"There is always sadness in love. Don't be afraid. You must be brave. *Féroce.*"

I was shivering and wished for a wool sweater. I wanted to run. But I did not. If I ran, he would be walking alone this dim night. With barely a sliver of moon. And the mist rising would soon cover the moon. The scene was terrifying and a little beautiful. I could not leave him there on an endless road. Soggy and sinking into bog. His head bare, mouthing her name. Mathilde. Half-blind, in despair, with no place to rest.

As ghosts buried into sepia
fog of night, worn hands, legs
stride between dread of trench
and dream—you walk

in silence, ask only legs
to pass over the barren ground
brown onto brown slow harrowing
rhythm of boots like a far-off drum

echoing wind, whistle, lark
a shell blazes, delivers swallowed
grief into darkness waiting

to be devoured.
The world soaked
pale, and still the light
held beyond all imagining.

I was trembling and crouched to the ground leaning on the cold granite of her tomb. She waved from the far end of the theatre. The way performers wave when the show has finished. I met her eyes. She was fading. Retreating. I didn't want to be alone here in the dark.

"*Au revoir, poète.*"

Slowly, as if waking from a dream, my eyes adjusted to the night. I was spellbound watching my own shadow. How would I find my way back to the gate, my bicycle, or the way home? She was sitting in her daybed. Her raft. Her feet dangling. Aged, poised, looking content. With her fountain pen she was sketching poppies, orchids, hyacinths. I was in the doorway. On the tips of the branches. And not quite the same. The delicate petals of the white roses I'd brought began to unfurl and fall, like halfmoons waning. The scent of anise lingered.

A text pinged on my iPhone loud as a whistle blowing. *Take the road all the way to the bottom, until you reach the gate. Turn right. Follow the gate all the way. I'm here.* René was here? I hardly noticed fog had rolled in. The moon was completely obscured. I couldn't make out the street. I couldn't see my own feet. I felt along the damp ground in vain for my pack to fetch my headlamp. The temperature had dropped. My jeans were wet from the dew. The bells of Notre-Dame were ringing again. Like a foghorn tolling.

"Alas, you must not forget the fresh air," she said. Her voice was fading. I strained my ears. "And flowers. You won't make any money as *une écrivaine.* Not real money."

As I waved, she uncapped the brandy, poured it into her coffee. "And never say no to a gift of brandy. *Jamais.*"

"You okay?" René asked when I arrived at the gate where I'd left my bike. "Let's go for a drink."

We cycled back in the direction of Notre-Dame, past shadows and the crazy frantic traffic of Paris. The city never sleeps. My hands braced the handlebars, legs pushed pedals, mind whirled. For the life of me I tried not to lose pace with René and his black jacket. The strands of his blond hair glittering under the lamp light, all I could see as we flew through the narrow winding streets. Taking the sidewalks when we could, we passed under fluttering leaves of linden trees and crossed the river over Pont Marie to Boulevard Saint Germain. All the ghosts of the ancients echoed through the *quartier*. Poems came to me like songs reverberating inside my head. I hurled myself through the City of Lights as night fell. Absorbing every groove.

OTHER VOICES, OTHER ROOMS

I slammed the door so hard behind me the roof shook. "Good-bye!" I yelled back at Mother and under my breath, *Screw you.* If I dared, I would have stood on the front porch and screamed. Though it wasn't my nature to make grand gestures, and anyway, my scarf had caught in the door and I couldn't move my head. Leaving wasn't going to be easy. My face was caught twisted upwards so that all I could see was the morning sky. Stained pink and orange. The shock of such beauty at that very moment overwhelmed me. I'm going to get through this. My anger left me like a sigh.

For months I have been overcome with emotion. What was really sweeping over me were my losses. And all that was passing me by. This all began when Mother moved in after Father passed away last year. A photograph, embroidered pillows, table clothes, the few things she brought with her, opening up faded memories and half-told stories. Dreams that were no more were returning to haunt me. I'm seventy years old and time is leaving me. It dawned on me that I should breathe in the light, and with what felt like a last gasp at freedom, I yanked my scarf until it came loose. Two voices were mounting a battle in me. One said stay and one said run away. What did any of this matter today anyway? I wasn't going any further than the greengrocer, where I go every Saturday morning.

Wind kicked up the leaves in the street. I'd left Mother inside with CBC radio on. For the past hour I'd been listening to an interview with that Italian Navy Commander who had rescued the migrant boats off of the island of Lampedusa, south of Sicily. It was as though he had not told the story before of how hundreds had died attempting to cross the Mediterranean Sea in overcrowded boats.

"I can't find the tea bags. Did you hide them again?" she asked.

"All those children choked on gas fumes," I said. Jesus almighty.

"Fine, fine. Off you go. I'll find them myself."

Tears dropped from my chin as I gripped my grocery bags. The steps to the sidewalk were slick with ice. I had been a dancer once. I should be able to float down the railing to the street below.

Listening to the quaking voice of the Italian Navy Commander as he re-told the story summoned memories for me that I'd thought long forgotten. After WWII, our family left Holland for Canada; I was three years of age, with Mother and Father on a boat from Rotterdam to Halifax. During the night the ship would make noises like it was alive, squeaking and bellowing. From my bunk, I could see a light on the deck and on windy nights when the ship heaved, I couldn't sleep. I'd set my eyes to that light and imagine our new home.

In Halifax, the church billeted us with a family with children my age and I'll never forget the way the mother greeted us or her fish and potato pie. I loved the crispy brown topping of that pie. She fed us extra servings trying to fatten us up. I didn't know, until years later, when I found a photograph taken on the day we arrived, that we all looked like we were starving. But we were among the fortunate ones. Father had a job waiting and soon the company moved us to Toronto.

Father wanted to talk about Holland before he died, but Mother wouldn't have it. She's been living with me since he passed away and she talks all the time now, following me around the kitchen like a robot that won't stop talking. "We were hungry, always hungry. You don't remember but your father cycled miles just for a bottle of milk and some onions."

Before Thanksgiving, I planted tulip bulbs in my garden. Three dozen Ballerinas this year. The package promised they would smell like mandarin oranges. You need something to look forward to.

I wasn't going far. I've lived forty years alone in my bungalow on Bathurst Street. The neighbours were all working-class people when I moved in. I ignored Mother's advice even then—"too many immigrants and too close to downtown."

The inflammation in my knees was especially painful this morning, and my whole body shuddered as my feet hit the pavement. Aching joints a reminder that Saturday mornings used to be for long rehearsals. At thirty, I was old to be given my first major role. Stravinsky's *Rites of Spring*. I knew it would be challenging. Then, only a week before opening night, I fell and tore my hamstring. There was a brilliant young dancer rising up in the company. That was all it took. She got Jesse Roland as a dance partner and I was put out to pasture from the work I loved.

Once down the steps I had the urge to demonstrate that I could still spin in circles, that my body remembered. But I caught myself and hurried on to the greengrocer.

My plan for dinner was to make a simple soup. I'll put a little something extra in it just to surprise myself. Mother will say it needs more salt and then she'll retell her stories like they happened yesterday. She can't remember my name or where the sugar bowl or the drawer with the spoons is, but after a lifetime of trying to leave the past behind, now she was unearthing painful memories, returning as though to her own house for the first time where there were other voices and other rooms. "These things you don't forget," she says, rapping her spoon against the side of her dinner plate. A house too loud to ignore.

As the whirl of the wind pulled the last of the leaves off the branches, my body began to loosen up, and I forgot for the moment how many years were behind me. The street was empty and quiet except for winter finches chirping up and down in high-pitched warbles. Just the right amount of song spritzing through the bare branches. One winter you see finches and the next you don't. But they've come back as though they had never left, with their little yellow heads and trilling sounds as I passed St. Helen's Church. I caught myself staring at homeless Benson asleep at the door covered over in a pile of dirty blankets. He'd been living on these church steps for ten years. I'll bring him a sweet on my way home. He'll never look me in the eye and we won't talk, but he'll reach for the sweet and I'll feel the warmth of his hands and wonder again where he came from.

Just then, a small bus stopped in the street and a group of girls disembarked, all in black leotards and white tights and wearing thin windbreakers. Not enough against the cold. There would be lessons this morning. They scattered up to the front porch of an old blue Victorian, their boots thumping on the steps like small deer hooves. I watched until the last one had gone inside.

I looked down at my tights, slipped and bunched at my thin ankles, pointed my toes, and kept walking the last few blocks to the grocer.

Two men arrived at the greengrocer the same time as me. The wind was blowing hard, echoing in the narrow street. It wasn't snowing but the forecast said it might. "You first," I said to the older gentleman. His toque was the colour of cantaloupe and skewed to one side. Swatches of stiff grey hair pushed out the sides of his hat like icicles. At the identical moment, the other man, enormously tall and wearing a knit turtleneck and no coat at all, waved his arm, "No, you first. Please." He was shivering, so we all squeezed comically through the door together.

The store was full of shoppers already: children, young people, old ones like me. An Asian woman squatted between two little girls in shiny fuchsia coats, unwrapped each of them a candy; something to keep them occupied while their mother shopped. The stooped Greek man I recognized from the neighbourhood where I see him walking his pug. He always says hello.

The windows of the store steamed up on the inside. A siren went off in the street, but no one seemed to notice. We followed the rows and shoved things into our baskets. It was a tiny bit of a store but rippled with sunlight despite the cold. And rattling from the speakers, so loud it couldn't be ignored, Led Zeppelin was playing "Immigrant Song." People swayed to the music like they'd found something they'd lost. An old guy with grey hair and bicycle knickers long out of style jerked his shoulders up and down when the song got to the *ah ah*. That's the kind of thing I might do if nobody was watching.

I looked for grapefruits, carrots, potatoes and cabbage, a bundle of mint if Ahmed, the shopkeeper, had any this time of year. I could sneak that into the soup or the salad. The aisles were crammed with jars from Thailand and China; chutneys from India, even Dutch *stroopwafel* cookies. Father used to drive across the city to buy those cookies at the Dutch store. They were special treats, I discovered, that he kept in his desk for days he needed a little cheering up.

A long line formed past the citrus fruits and bananas. I liked looking at the expensive things by the line-up to the checkout; dates and figs, persimmon and quince, like small treasures. Cape gooseberries from Columbia and star fruit from the Philippines. Jeepers, the whole world was getting blended together. Then I saw a package at eye level that looked fresh from a bakery. I leaned towards the thick long roll of doughy flatbread, folded over like a blanket, covered in spices, protruding out of an oily brown paper bag. I reached out to touch the puffed up paper. It was warm and I imagined tasting the crust. I considered asking Ahmed where it came from when I laid my hands on the paper. Warm and supple as breasts.

I never slept with Jesse Roland. I should have done. I shuddered at the memory of the two of us, half naked and groping feverishly, until someone banged on the door of the change room and we hurried off in opposite directions. I pulled the package off the shelf and slipped the soft bread inside my coat. Patted the buttons and tightened my belt like I'd just filled a cavity. A hole I hadn't known was there. A bell sounded and wind swept in when the door opened and closed. Was someone watching me the whole time? At the till, the guy in front emptied his basket. Shiitake mushrooms, ricotta cheese, asparagus and a bundle of green leaves. "Ricotta and tortellini with crispy *funghi* tonight," he said to tall thin Ahmed at the counter.

"And what are those green leaves?" I wanted to ask but didn't dare. The warm bread in the shiny paper had slipped under my belt like a freshly caught trout. I pushed it back into place with my thumb, inching it above my belt buckle.

"Bergamot. I sprinkle the table," he said to Ahmed, as if reading my mind.

The fresh bread pressed into my belly like lovers spooning. With our woolly hats and scarves covering us over, were we different people than we were used to being? I searched for something to look at as I waited my turn at the checkout. The front of a magazine or a newspaper. I was warming and on the wild edge of my mind, I had the urge to unbutton my coat. Throw off everything. The old man was taking too long time to tell Ahmed his story. The bread was going to land on my feet.

"My wife was trained as a cellist. The St. Petersburg Philharmonic and then in America, she was a star. Unforgettable."

Some people were so clever and talented. The heat of the bread travelled across my chest like I was an oven. My face was flushed so much so that the rest of me began to shiver. Were Ahmed's eyes following me? I shifted from one foot to the other.

By the time Ahmed finished ringing in the man's groceries, I was shoulder to shoulder with the enormous guy who came into the store at the same time. We were at the side-by-side checkouts. We smiled at each other. He had a gaping brown paper stuffed with a long roll of the crusty bread in his basket. There were eggplants, tomatoes, cucumber, onions and thick yogurt. Mint too. I felt my belly as I stared into his basket. Lord, what had I done?

"It's so small this store, but everything is here," he said with a smile. "All the brightly coloured foods I love. People misunderstand us, we make food to remember. We cook together, we sing and share food with our friends. We make salads and small plates with cucumber and sweet tomato, fresh parsley and mint. Dressed simply with olive oil and lemon. Generously salted."

My stomach was rumbling. I didn't budge.

"And a delicious satisfying yogurt and eggplant dish with tomatoes," he said. "Tart and sweet."

Like a lifeline in a storm, he was clinging to his past. I didn't know what to say. With my free hand, I pushed aside the buttons of my coat feeling for the warm bulge of the bread. And then my voice startled me, reaching into the room like I was calling out for forgiveness. "I'm going to make soup. And after, I'll slice the grapefruit and sprinkle it with the mint." I put my carry bags on the counter. "So," I said, "what do you do with that bread?"

"This naan? I rub in oil," he said. He closed his eyes, his head swayed from side to side. "Cumin and oregano. Garlic; you can't have too much garlic." He flashed the fingers of one hand twice. "Bake in the hot oven for ten. And if you're lucky you have some left in the morning."

Waves of scents flowed out of the warm paper into the space between us. I almost pulled the bread out from my coat to pay for it.

"Where are you from?" I asked, fearing my boldness would offend.

"I'm Syrian," the man said. He didn't seem to mind my question. "We are here three months. I love Canada, but it's very cold. They gave me a coat, but it was not big enough," he laughed. He pointed to the grapefruit in my basket. "We eat mint with everything. But not that." He smiled at me, paid for his groceries.

Then he turned back, touched my basket. "Why not join us? Bring your family. The more the better." He threw his arms up and down purposefully, filling in the spaces. When people arrive here, they've given up everything. You never know what they did before. He might have been a conductor of a famous orchestra.

My mind flooded with the blasting music of Lynyrd Skynyrd's "Free Bird," the scent of his salty skin and the spicy bread, and smells of an engine, bilge, and smoke from a ship I barely remembered, carrying Dutch immigrants across the Atlantic Ocean more than sixty years ago. And the dance partner that came and left before we began. I wanted to leap into his arms. Take me home with you. My voice fell to a whisper. "Thank you, but no. I can't."

"Here," he said. "Take the bread. My gift to you. When we share bread, we are all family." Then he was gone. I forgot to ask his name. I piled my purchases into my carry bags. Then I made my way back into the store, past the other shoppers waiting to pay, to the shelf with the warm bread. I pried the package out from inside my coat and laid it back on the stack. Trying to unthief myself. Was God watching? I was giving it back.

On the way home I passed St. Helen's Church and Benson awake on the steps folding his blankets. I pulled off a large piece of the bread with a swatch of brown paper, walked over and placed the warm naan in his hand. "Thank you," he said. He looked me in the eye. It unnerved me and I felt like ducking behind a cedar hedge. But I'm too old for that. I looked right back at him. The sun was overhead and in the light he looked young, like someone's son. He could have been my son. I smiled. He had already turned back to the work of folding his blankets.

At dinner, Mother helped me set the table. I placed the cutting board with slices of the bread on the tablecloth. Our hands met as I placed the salt on the table. "Mint on grapefruit. That's a little weird," she said. "But that bread looks good. Is that Greek? I'd like to go to Greece. You know, before I die."

After dinner, I picked up the soup bowls and walked into the kitchen. Mother stayed at the table and drifted off to sleep gripping the edge of the tablecloth. The door closed behind me without a sound. Already it was dark outside. I dropped my head over the pot of leftover soup trying to smell a past that I wanted to remember. There was the naan bread lying on the cutting board, with the aroma of some place I'd never been before, and of a man so tall with dancing hands, who was in his new home somewhere preparing a feast. I closed my eyes and could hear the wind whirling up outside. Hail was tapping the window like tiny stars asking to come inside. "Ah ah," I sang over the soup. "Ah ah," over the slices of naan bread. My shoulders rose and fell, the room swayed.

Somewhere in another room, a dancer began to spin to the gusting rhythms of Igor Stravinsky. Her hands fluttered free as a wild bird unwinding into the night. A single strand of moonlight cast her plumage golden, setting her afire, and then she was gone. The dazzling firebird escaped from the small lit kitchen on Bathurst Street, took flight over a ship docking in Halifax harbour, soared above the port city of Rotterdam, set free into the snowy sparkling dark of this night.

A Love Supreme

"And therefore is Love said to be a child,
Because in choice he is so oft beguiled."
—*A Midsummer Night's Dream*

Jacob

Sunday morning on the verge of spring, I awoke to the earth slowly drying out, and all of the anticipation of a spring that had come late, but finally arrived. The kind of day that was heavy with purpose. For weeks the rain had been relentless, pouring over the cedar tops, Douglas firs, and lodgepole pines. Birds in the woods around my house had been clattering so loudly I finally gave up on sleep and descended the stairs to the sitting room. I made myself a cup of strong black tea, turned on the radio, took my seat by the window. On the plane coming in from Detroit last night, my heart had been racing and my nerves jumpy. As I always do, I pulled my chair closer to the window, letting sunlight cover me over. But the dogs wouldn't settle. Both were agitated: circling my chair, sniffing by the rear door, staring at me. Expecting something.

Down the yard, barely visible behind the trees and grasses grown high and let go over the years, was the shed where I stored my bow. I'd been content to let the shed slowly be swallowed by foliage. It had been so many years, rats or mice may have gnawed through the quiver. Truth is, that bow has rarely left my thoughts. I have been living in shame and isolation. What had I made of the gift bequeathed to me?

"I don't think you're done." The raspy smoker's voice of that old man in Detroit, wheezing tar and resins, was ringing in my ears like tinnitus: Those were the last words he said to me. I shuddered at the sight of that shed and the thought of re-opening it after all these years.

The tenor sax of John Coltrane's A Love Supreme was blowing through the room. I drank my tea, followed the fluttering melody, tried to forget my worries. People expected too much of Coltrane. Everything he suffered was in this piece; his troubled life set him on his spiritual journey, and eventually to his faith in God. Then I quickly got lost. The suite became complex, Coltrane chanting, a love supreme, over and over, was irritating me and I wondered if he'd solved anything. The slant of sunlight and the wafting horn should be consoling, but they were not. I wished it were raining again. Seattle's greyness would better suit my mood. If I were a drinker I would pour something stronger into my teacup.

At this moment, I settled my frailness onto my mat, lit incense, closed my eyes, went into a meditation. Soaring above my life like an eagle with its keen eyesight, I flew above goodness and righteousness. On pockets of air I rose and descended. All things fall. This is not the world I wanted. I summoned an image of Kristen. She'd been in Seattle for half a year now, tending to her dying mother and consoling her father. Her husband, Nathan, back home in San Francisco. There would be nothing wrong with this, except that the old woman had been cruel to her. Placing her with that couple all those years ago was a fault on my part. Playing God. It wasn't right.

At this stage of my life, I should be reflecting back on my good deeds, not my regrets. You can't expect to get everything right in life. But I should have made Grandfather proud. I owed him that. He had such hopes for me. Gone now, but I was sure he could see my mistakes. It's frightening how things go, and how quickly time passes. Now I was the one long in the tooth, with sore hips and aching joints. Even lifting my teacup, I laboured. It was questionable whether I could even manage to hold my bow hand steady. How grandfather trusted me with his bow when I was just seventeen. Serious and ceremonial that day. "You will change the world, Jacob." The way my chest grew puffy. I was thrilled when he spoke my name. As though I were his missing son. And I would move mountains.

We had been working together in his study, revising for my Latin exam, when he closed the text, walked to the cupboard, and took down the long narrow case. He pulled me close, and we stared together at the slender hand-carved wooden bow and the round quiver with three arrows. He was about to give to me, an ordinary boy, abandoned by my own parents, his cherished possession. He pulled one of the arrows from the quiver and placed it in my hand. Light shone through the window. Some things in life are magical and happen only once. I knew nothing of arrows and could not tell if the faded ivory coloured tips were of bone or horn. Grandfather was frail then and his voice was barely audible: "There are people who need love. Who suffer for what they have not been given. This bow is your instrument. It is with you now."

Light washed through the open window over the length of the bow. The study grew quiet. It seemed impossible, these words he spoke. My heart swelled, thunderous. I was to be a warrior.

After school the next day, I carried the case to the back of the house and took the path into the woods. I sat on the forest floor, on the densely packed moss, and arranged the case on the ground in front of me. When I was sure no one was watching, I opened the lid, leaned forward, my fingers stroked the bow. Eager to see what it would do. Nothing happened. Grandfather had said the bow was meant for love. That was all I knew.

Going into the woods with the bow became a habit. Even on rainy and overcast days, I carried the bow case with me into the forest. It was never gloomy: ferns and lichen, young trees and old growth towered to the canopy, light trickled down, flooding me over, giving the act a kind of pleasing celebration. No doubt encouraging me to go a little further than the day before. I'd take the bow into my hands, examine the string and the nock, the curve and the belly. Then I'd hold the grip, testing the sight, and the tautness of the bowstring. Eventually, I'd rest it against the trunk of a tree and stare at it, mystified by its simple beauty, and understanding nothing.

One day, I was sitting cross-legged, working the smooth fetching of an arrow through my fingers. I wondered what would happen if I pushed the tip of the arrow into my ankle. After so many days of nothing working, without a thought of the consequences, I became fixated, and had to do it. I rolled up my pant leg and punctured myself. A flash glowed from the spot where the tip penetrated my skin, like a shooting star, startling me. My ankle began to fill with warmth. I was sure I was bleeding but could see no blood. The tip of the arrow had made no wound, no mark of any kind. Then, like a summery glow, heat flooded through me until I was pleasantly relaxed and content. I had to know more so I pressed the tip into the inside of my wrist. Light flashed again, stronger light than before. Long rays split into shards and shot into the sky like tiny stars. I should have finished there, but I couldn't stop. I had to go further. All caution gone from me, I grabbed hold of the arrow and shoved the point into my heart, pushing with all my force, until the shaft was made crooked. In an instant, as though a torch had been lit to a fuse, a great light burst open. My hand still holding the shaft trembled. Why I didn't recoil, I don't know. My heart was forced open until there was no inside or outside. Only light. Bedazzling light.

I was sprawled on the ground weeping and knew I had passed out. I stretched my legs and my arms and ran my hands over my chest. I was confused, hungry, and wondered how much time had passed. I glanced around for the broken arrow but couldn't see it. I became panicky, crawling on my hands and knees, I pushed through the undergrowth, searching for a long while. I was shivery and sure it was late. Grandfather would be expecting me. So, I placed the quiver and the two remaining arrows back into the case with the bow, closed the lid, and scrambled to my feet. Three arrows seemed insufficient to change the world. I had already used up one.

Now I need someone to talk to. I have been carrying a secret for such a long time. A lifetime. I consider myself an honest man. I set out to do only good. I had no other purpose. My bow was intended simply as an instrument of love. Of course, I took a risk when

I shot the second arrow. I was young then and inexperienced. But well intentioned. Intention doesn't account for anything when you make a mistake. After that, I lost my nerve. I walked away from the gift Grandfather bestowed on me and away from my own shortcomings.

Kristen

Thank goodness the sun was shining this morning. April can be so gloomy in Seattle. I couldn't sleep and decided to go for a walk. The streets were empty, even in the U District. I took a detour by the neo-classical Carnegie Library just to have a reminder of how beautiful a building can be. The only place that looked open so early was Starbucks in the university village, so I headed there, and took a seat facing the window to sit in the sunlight.

I've been in Seattle six months, since my father called me to come home. Not my real dad. The one who adopted me when I was three. I was unnerved by his voice on the telephone that day, smooth and convincing. "Your mother needs you, Kristen. She's dying." Nothing like the thin, worn-out old man I found when I arrived. With one phone call he threw a wrench into my life. It's incredible what someone can ask for. I should have said no. She ruined my life. She's nobody to me. But I didn't.

I'd been living a simple, contented life in Berkeley, married to Nathan, who still takes me by the hand when we walk, after twenty-five years. Not a bad gig. I made partner last year at Amis and Associates, the most respected structural engineering company in the Bay Area. Loved and successful. The two things that are supposed to make for a happy life. But with that one phone call an old wound was re-opened. I reached through the telephone and reassured my father. "Tell her I'll come," I said. As though old fences could always be mended.

Since then, I have been here, sub-letting a garden level apartment in the U District, within walking distance of my childhood home. I have been nursing Mother and propping up Father's spirits. But today, the sun was shining. What a relief.

It was quiet in Starbucks when I arrived, but it was soon busy and someone had turned up the Fleet Foxes' *Helplessness Blues* on the sound system. Robin Pecknold's voice sounded like coffee percolating on a campfire and it was making me homesick. I scrolled through the photos on my iPhone, searching for one in particular, of Nath and me in Point Reyes Park last October. I remembered the fog was lifting, and we'd stopped to look east, back at the city. The red towers of the Golden Gate Bridge breaking through the mist.

Sitting at the counter, sipping my coffee, I began sketching a new development for the Berkeley brickyard. Something that would climb up through the fog would look amazing. I was excited again about what I was going to do when I got back to work.

I drew with my entire case of Derwent pencils sprawled on the counter, and texted Nathan. He was at the San Francisco airport waiting for his flight to Seattle. *First stop, Magnolia Park, to see the bald eagles,* I typed. It had been a month since we'd been together.

The time had come. I was heading over to Mother and Father's house first to make Mother some breakfast. Then I would tell her plainly, it's time for me to go. I'll explain there is a nurse coming tomorrow. She won't hear me. All she does is sleep. The closest we ever got to a conversation was last week when I raised her head as she spit up into a little cardboard bucket. I held her upright and stroked her hair. She was so small and frail I wondered, What had I been rebelling against all those years ago? Then the lights went out. In that moment, when we were both plunged into darkness, Mother began to cry. I cried too, sobbing like a child.

The music in Starbucks was beginning to grate on me. I gathered up my pencils, one by one into the metal case, and exited into the street, my thoughts with Nath and Magnolia Park.

Jacob

To understand my dilemma, I have to take you back, nearly fifty years ago now, when Kristen was three years old and living with her dad in a suburb of Detroit. He had been working on the assembly line at General Motors. Her mom was killed in a freak accident in the front yard of their home. After bingo one night, it was icy, and she'd slipped getting out of her best friend's car. Her best friend backed over her.

I was a young man then, living alone in a little flat in the University District of Seattle, and unfocused in my studies. My beloved grandfather had passed away a year earlier. I was halfway through a degree in Philosophy and Religion and had a part-time job baking bread at the Sunflower Bakery and Coffee Shop, owned by a man named Matt Morgan, who became my friend.

In good weather I would ride my bicycle along the viaduct on my way to work, admiring the young students, all rushing to class. It was the '50s, men wore ties, jackets, and long coats. The women were dressed elegantly too. There was confidence in the air. All of us excited about the future and trying to enhance our lives.

After Grandfather died, I found he had a box filled with names and addresses. There were letters from people who had written him, asking for help. Pasted inside the cover of the box was a note he had written to me about my parents leaving. It was a period of our lives Grandfather rarely spoke of. *They were early hippies, leaving America to travel the Overland to India. Searching for something. It was the times, Jacob. It will be hard for you to make sense of it. They lived in their own world. After they left for London, I never saw or heard from them again.*

Something began growing in me that day. It was like a sign. This box of letters had something to do with the bow. What happened to children when their parents left? What was it these people were hoping Grandfather might do for them? I got obsessed and pulled out every letter that had to do with children until they were piled neatly on the side of my desk and began to answer each one. I wrote letter after letter on yellow legal pads. That moment I wanted to start a home for children whose parents were gone or not up to the task.

No one replied until one day I received a handwritten scrawl on a tiny piece of paper.

There's been an accident. My child has no mother now. She needs someone who can give her a better life. Can you promise her that?

Many things are mixed up in my memory but this much is clear—my friend Matt Morgan knew a nice couple who were trying to adopt a baby. The man had just graduated law. The woman, an English major, was still at university and studying to be a teacher. The two of them had become friends at university and that spring they had just been married.

So, I stowed my bow in my duffel bag and the next day I took the train from Seattle to Detroit to meet the man who'd written the note.

"If she will have a better life," he said again and again, as we sat together in his little kitchen at the rear of the house. It was more like an interrogation. A bare, too-bright light bulb swung over the Formica tabletop as he drilled me. He was wearing a baseball cap with a capital D, crudely polished pointy boots, and a t-shirt with an American flag on the front. His fingers, stained yellow from nicotine, were wrapped around a cup of black coffee, and jittery. Over by the sink I could see several empty bottles of Jack Daniel's and by the back door, crushed boxes and a cluster of empties. There was something in his manner that made me suspect that there may have been booze in that coffee cup. He looked me straight in the eye in a way that unnerved me. We talked late through the night and into the early morning. He explained that his daughter was smart. "She should live in a nice suburb, like Bloomfield Hills. With good schools. Safe. No drugs. She could go to the University of Michigan in Ann Arbour. She's university material. And what am I?"

A damn alcoholic. His house, a little scrappy wooden structure with no lawn. I took a sip of coffee from the mug he'd put in front of me and began to explain who the new parents would be. I was talking too quickly, trying to speed everything up to get out of there. I fiddled with the buttons of my coat and tried not to look rushed. "They are a nice young couple from Seattle. The man has just finished law school and the woman is studying to be a teacher."

He was nodding. "She's intelligent," he said, "you can see it already. She gets herself dressed up in my wife's clothes and throws herself around the room singing and dancing. And come look at this thing she's built out of blocks." He dragged me into the front room to show me an elaborate set-up with building blocks and bric-a-brac that was laid out on the carpet.

"That's a whole damn city. High-rises, houses, and bridges, and look, even little trees." It wasn't like he was bragging. I could see he was mesmerized. In the end, it was the couple's education that cinched it. He pulled a pink plastic cup from the sink, wiped it with a rag, and dropped it into a brown paper shopping bag. Then he went back to the living room, and began stuffing toys, a cardigan, a little knitted hat into the bag.

He was distracted, so I returned to the kitchen and swiftly pulled my bow from my canvas sack. I was determined to sneak upstairs and shoot an arrow into the child. Within seconds I was at the door of her room. It was my first time shooting anyone other than myself. I was terrified. I had to take a leap of faith. She was sleeping. I drew back my bow and propelled an arrow in her direction. Twisting into an arc, it transformed into a beam of light, releasing hundreds of tiny stars as it plunged into her heart. Now she would love her new parents. I was sure of it.

When the father returned to the kitchen, I was back, seated at the table, my bag zipped. He handed me the little girl, bundled in a blanket, along with the shopping bag stuffed with her things. She was awake and her small round eyes followed me. I suddenly felt relieved. He walked me to the front door, leaned his face tightly against the blanket without saying a word, then he opened the front door of his house and pointed me out.

On the long train trip back to Seattle with the child, I could not get out of my head the image of her dad, bloodshot eyes, holding his head crying. "My whole life is over," he said. "She's been robbed of her life, too." A couple of times I had felt the leg of the table trembling. I had done what I thought was right.

When she woke up to the sweet rhythm of the train rocking along the track, I said something stupid to her, that I was like a minister, and that her father had asked me to look after her. I should have discussed with him what he wanted me to say. I suddenly felt responsible and unprepared for a three-year-old with a brown paper bag and her whole future in my hands. I picked up the bag and placed it on the seat beside us. There was a stuffed bunny, some clothes, the cup, and diapers. Diapers for a three-year-old? It was too late now to ask for instructions.

She said, "hungry," so I ordered her toast with a soft-boiled egg. Then I sang to her—Cole Porter's "All of You." I did not know what else to do. She had been watching my mouth and by the third time through, she joined in and sang with me. Other than that, she did not speak a word until we arrived home.

Suddenly, I had this child with me, two thousand miles from her home. This shows you how blind-sided I was. I was confident I was doing the right thing.

I sent a telegram to the couple the next day. They were surprised and delighted that they had been chosen. When I brought the little girl, Kristen, to their flat, a small rented room, above Woolworth's five-and-ten-cents, the man made a little speech and we clinked glasses of apple wine.

Kristen

One day, when we were still living in the apartment over top of the department store—I would have been six or seven then—that minister visited us. He had a kind face, with blue eyes that were as bright as dancing musical notes. He had shiny hair and he smoked a pipe, which looked funny but smelled amazingly sweet like a Christmas candle. I drew a picture of him when he was talking to Mother. I asked to build something with him, but Mother said my building blocks were put away. So, I sat on the edge of the sofa looking at my book instead. Mother had tied a big red bow in my hair. I felt silly, all dressed up with a bow stuck on the top of my head. So, I read my book. He was humming a song softly. *I love all of you,* I sang to myself. I wondered if he was my real dad.

Jacob

I see things. When I am deep in my meditations, I will suddenly be pulled into a scene. The couple I gave Kristen to should have been happy with the little girl. I watched them as they sat up late, invited friends over, smoked cigarettes, and griped. "Geoffrey Higgins and his wife have a flat with a living room and a television set," said the wife. "Jack Robertson bought a house in the suburbs with a pool," said the husband. They had difficulty at first, the new father commuting long hours to work by bus, the mother still in school, and the little girl was often left with a neighbour lady who took in children. I wanted to step in then, but you have to trust that in time things will change. It's easy to forget that everyone struggles in the beginning.

The day I visited, the girl was sitting alone reading a children's book called *The Ballerina Bunny*. She stretched her neck and pointed her toes. Then she snuck a look at me, and in a voice sweet as a songbird she sang "All of You" and went back to her book. After that it was impossible for me to focus on anything else. The mother impressed on me that the father was working but the wages were low, that affordable housing was hard to come by and they hoped to one day buy a house in the suburbs. "Ballet classes are expensive," she said, and they could not afford to enroll the girl. "Money doesn't fall out of the sky."

A few years later, I saw something horrible. I was not brave enough to try to fix it. I had no idea what to do. There was no one to report to. Who else was going to take her at this stage?

I called Matt Morgan. I had to talk to someone discreetly. I hadn't slept for weeks. I was frustrated and angry. This is when I learned the limits of my powers. I could start something, but I couldn't finish it. I remembered everything about that conversation. The coldness of the air as we walked. It was probably a sunny day somewhere, up high, but fog had dropped over the city, everything grey. The trees were bare, steely looking. I tried to control my anger. My own culpability. We walked past the pier, gazing out at the freighters sitting low in the harbour. The foghorn blew relentlessly.

"I should have saved her life," I said. "Her father expected that of me."

"Those were difficult years. Unwed mothers gave their children up then. Widowed fathers too. It was a different time, Jacob. You can't fix everything."

I didn't mention my bow. I'd just given up my pipe, and I was fidgety, and my nerves were edgy. I don't think he would have believed me anyway. "You're talking about her like you think you're her father. You're not." We walked in silence then. There was something wrong with the way I'd done it. When I shot her, she was sleeping. Then, as he handed her to me, she woke, we looked each other in the eyes. I would have been the first person she saw. Was this the way it worked? The arrow made you love the first person you saw? I glanced over at Matt. He was striding along the boardwalk like he didn't have a care in the world. The weather was warming up. The coat I was wearing was too heavy. I felt in my pocket and was relieved to find a packet of gum. A family with a little boy passed by us. The boy looked up at the dad, who picked him up then, and hoisted him onto his shoulders.

Kristen

I left home when I was seventeen. I couldn't get out of there fast enough. In those days, 1973, no one I knew back in Seattle had moved out or was going anywhere. There I was, scholarship in hand, driving a rusty orange Vega, the worst car General Motors ever built, but it was the only thing I could find for five hundred bucks, south to San Francisco to start engineering classes at UC Berkeley. That car guzzled gas, burned oil and began overheating on the Golden Gate Bridge. I made my way over to the right lane and somehow exited the bridge, stopped at a gas station, filled up the leaky radiator, put five bucks worth of gas in the car and carried on through San Francisco and over the Bay Bridge to Berkeley, singing "Steamroller" along with James Taylor on the radio. Within the week I had a part-time job and took a suite over top of Hink's Department Store.

Then, I admit, I went a little wild. One night I was at a party, high on mescaline, and there was acid in the punch bowl, too, and I don't know what else. I had sex with a guy on a mattress on the floor in one of the rooms. It was dark except for the light of the moon through the curtainless window. He looked okay. Except that he didn't say anything. Not one word. The sex was fast, the way you pop off a beer cap and guzzle the whole thing in one long chug. Slap the bottle back down on the counter with a little foam on your lips and a smile. *Ahhh.* Done. He came in me, and partly on my leg as he pulled himself out. Yanked up his pants and exited the room. Lying there on that mattress, that was a reckless *aha* moment for me. This sounds unbelievable, but it woke me up. My first year at Berkeley and I'd gotten myself pregnant. With the help of the Women's Health Collective and a kindly professor, who could see I was smart, I put myself on track.

When I turned nineteen, a small stipend arrived in the mail from a law office in Michigan. For your education, was all the note said. From an uncle I never knew, who for some reason decided to help me out. I was curious who he was and wrote to the lawyer. He wrote back, saying only that the uncle wished to remain anonymous. I wondered then, if it was the nice man with the shiny hair and musical blue eyes, who smelled like Christmas.

In my final year of Engineering School, I met Nathan, a journalism major. He smoked a pipe and wore a funny little wool hat with a brim, which was endearing to me. I was shy with him right from the start. He was well over six feet tall, lean as a pencil and he made me think of a sunflower the way he always faced the goodness in things. He wore his hair long, and it flipped into a curl at his shoulders like Jackson Browne on the cover of the album *Saturate Before Using.*

Jacob

When Kristen left home, I was convinced she would be free. Meanwhile, back in Seattle, the parents got all the breaks. They grew rich. You'd think when people do well they would share but in fact the reverse is true. They had dinner parties, bought expensive antiques, travelled, and went on cruises. Months and years went by when they almost never telephoned Kristen.

Kristen

Marriages are weird things. Two of my friends got married after graduation. I was a bridesmaid for my friend, who got married in Big Sur, with eight guests. Not one of them from her family. Exactly what she wanted. This got Nathan and me talking marriage too. The next thing I knew, we were talking about where we'd have our ceremony and who we would invite. It was the first time I told him about Mother.

"If you're going to spend the rest of your life with me, you may as well know the truth," I said.

"Did she hurt you?"

"She did. When Dad wasn't home. Kicked me with the heel of her shoe. Or she'd take a swing at the back of my head. One day she knocked me to the floor and kicked me over and over, screaming. I never trusted her after that. Never told her anything important to me. Dad just kind of ignored me when he came home. In a way, he hurt me more."

In the end, we invited them and they came. They arrived the morning of the wedding and went back to Seattle the next day. Mother wore a mini dress and mingled among our friends shaking hands like a politician. They all loved her. And Father acted like a complete cuckoo, telling stupid jokes. I couldn't wait for them to go home.

Then I didn't hear from my parents for years. Gradually my memories of my life with them faded. Until one night, when they would have been old, Father telephoned and begged me to come home to Seattle. "She's dying, Kristen."

That night, lying in bed, Nathan and I fought about what we should do.

"I told Dad I was coming."

"You should have said no," Nathan said. "I don't get it. You walked away from them twenty years ago. They don't give a damn about you. Then suddenly you want to nurse your mother."

"I'm afraid not to go."

"Seriously?"

"She's going to die."

"Well, I don't think there's anything up in Seattle but heartache."

Then Nathan said something he had not said in a long time. "I wish we had kids of our own. Then you wouldn't go. We'd be your family."

There were not many topics we circled but could not touch. But this one, the sadness of no children, was like rain forest moss spreading over the roof of me.

"We can't change the past, Nath."

"That's exactly what you're trying to do. What about us?"

Neither of us spoke. Under the covers his hand reached for me. I had folded my arms and legs into my chest, making myself small. The decision had been made. He slid beside me under the crumpled bedding and pushed his face up against my back and kissed my shoulder. Two weeks later we packed the car and I drove up the coast to Seattle.

I did not recognize my mother at first. She was withered and frail looking. In the beginning, Father sat with Mother every day. Then every other day. Eventually, he barely entered her room at all, leaving her care to me. He took walks alone or sat in his study reading.

Amid a blur of nursing, administering medication, feeding, slow walks with a walker and trying to calm Father's teary outbursts, six months went by. I don't know what happened with Nath and me. We weren't fighting. We hardly spoke. He said I was slipping away.

One Sunday morning, we walked over to the house together. Nath had just flown in early, and he sat out on the rear deck reading, waiting for me. As I fumbled with the lid of a pill bottle for Mother, I noticed how the living room had taken on a nursing home smell. Sweaty and medicinal. Mother was asleep and Father was dozing in his chair. I opened the back door for some air. Dappled sunlight was drying the wet deck from the night's rain. It was warm and finally felt like spring.

"They're both resting. This is the strangest thing," I said, leaning back against the warming wood of the deck. "Even now, when Mother is near the end of her life, and she can't say a word I can understand, she's complaining. She must have regrets she wants to unburden."

Tiny birds flitted about in the trees, rustling the thin branches. "Finches perhaps," Nathan said. "Stirring now that the sun is out." "Right," I said. "Nath, I want to shake her like a rattle. Give us a chance to mend."

"It's too late for that, Kris. You want her to say sorry. Some people can't say sorry."

"I just want to fix things between us."

"Everything can't be fixed."

I looked up at the trees, light with new leaf, whirling in the breeze. "Sometimes, when I'm sitting with her at night, I envision a steel span bridge and I want to un-build it, piece by piece, until nothing remains of my life with her."

"You're tired," he said. "And your mom is stubborn."

"I'm stubborn too, thinking I could change her now."

"Just sit with her. You don't have to talk. I'm going for a walk," he said.

"I love you, Nath. I've screwed up everything. Haven't I?"

"Love you, too. See you about noon then?"

"Yes. Magnolia Park to see the bald eagles."

I went into the den, which was Mother's room now that she couldn't take the stairs. She was asleep so I sat in the chair beside the bed listening to her breathing. Then I began. I said everything I was thinking. "Who is my dad? What happened to my mom? Why didn't you love me?"

She lay on the bed, curled onto her side, her small mouth opened and closed. Her breath rose and fell. She opened her mouth wide like a bird waiting for the mother to give some food. I propped her up, held a cup to her mouth. Water spilled down her chin.

Jacob

I have not slept for weeks. This was not the outcome I wanted for Kristen. Back then, so many years ago now, I was playing God. The couple seemed decent. They were desperate for a child. I could not have foreseen what was going to happen, it's true. But I sacrificed this girl. There is no peace for me in this. Now I have to fix my mistake. I don't know what I should do, but I'll not resurrect my bow.

This all started up again when Kristen's biological father, back in Detroit, contacted me. I had not heard from him in all these years. He said he wanted to ask me something. He was getting on and believed he was near the end. Would I come? I wanted to take the train again. Go slowly. I was in no rush to deliver sad news. But there is no train now between Seattle and Detroit. So, I flew.

"Is she happy?" he asked. He poured us each a glass of scotch. I didn't touch mine. The atmosphere seemed too intimate. It was almost morning. I hadn't slept yet. I was scrolling through my memory siphoning off all the horrible bits, trying to recall something worthy but true. I looked into his grave face. We could compare notes on how we had both given her away.

"I want to hear about her life," he said. His voice sounded like a Harley-Davidson with no muffler. Pop-pop pause. The blinds were open, and the room became incredibly light.

"She's brave," I said. "And strong. Beautiful and kind." I told him about Nathan, and that they loved each other. He asked me a lot of questions. I felt sick. I could not look him in the eye. Finally, in a quiet voice I barely recognized as my own, I retold her story. With every word I tore open a sore. There was never a point when he interrupted. I kept going, unburdening myself. Before I knew it, I told him about the arrow.

He leaned back on the couch. He was wiry and he seemed remarkably sharp for his age. His face was composed but I could see his shoulders had slumped. He was fingering the length of his walking stick, rubbing the staff over and over with his crooked fingers until I had the feeling it was a loaded gun. I was desperate for air. He spoke clearly. In the slightest way, he looked wounded.

"Is that all? I don't think you're done."

"No," I said. An apology would have been insulting.

"If you did it before, you can do it again. Get it right this time."

"You are her patron?" I asked. "The uncle?"

"Of course, I sent the money," he said. "Son of a bitch. For a smart guy, you're kind of dim-witted."

He rose to his feet and shook my hand. "Time means a lot to me."

"It's risky," I said.

"Every venture involves risk," he said. He'd been drinking and he looked tired and testy.

"I understand."

"I don't think you're done," he said, as he shut the door.

When I got home to Seattle, I was tired but could not sleep; I lay in my bed listening to the rain on the tin roof of my little house, a drum beating out my past. By morning, the sun was up and the earth slowly drying out. The birds were noisy, flitting among the branches, and the dogs circled the room unable to settle. My thoughts were drifting wildly. I'm going to be eighty in a few months. I don't have a lot of time. Something else was grating on me too. My own heart was not right.

I woke from my meditation like I was waking from a miracle. A whole lifetime had passed. At least that's how it seemed. Sunlight swept through the room. I slumped back into my chair. Coltrane's *A Love Supreme* was still playing on the radio. They were playing the whole thing. The melody was comforting to me now. "Miles Davis gave him the biggest break of his life. And then had to fire him because he couldn't quit the drugs and booze," the announcer said. "*A Love Supreme* was Coltrane's response to the lowest point in his life, and his spiritual awakening."

If I have any strength left in my arms, I can't wait any longer. Memory is not without its shortcomings, but as I walked to the end of the garden to the shed where I'd stowed my bow, I knew I had to do this. The door was swollen and warped. Moss had grown, sealing the opening, like soggy cotton batten. I clicked through the numbers on the combination lock, surprising myself that I had not forgotten the action; right, left and right and again. I was rushed with an exhilaration I was not prepared for. As though, at last, I was unlocking the mystery. It was a long time ago I stowed my bow and the last arrow in the shed. I was ready to give up my power then and lead a simple life. I'd not given my bow a single thought until I sat with the old man in Detroit. It is unsophisticated by today's standards. Back then, I had counted myself lucky to possess these resources.

I wish to undo everything I've done. I mean this. It wasn't until I began rubbing off dust, cobwebs, and dead insects, cleaning and tightening the string, seeing it vibrate back to life, that I felt my bow return to me. Now I must right the wrong. What remains is hers, and hers alone. She has a right to love. I must be smart. Not too sentimental. Everything hinges on my accuracy. I have only one arrow remaining in my quiver, and two hearts to find.

I saw that the arrow was good. Still straight and true. I polished the shaft, fluffed the feather fetching and for good luck, spit on the head. About to take this road for the third time, I picked up my bow and quiver, stashed them in my duffle bag, and walked in the direction of Magnolia Park.

As I reached the park, the sun was overhead. I walked through the madrona trees to the bluffs overlooking Puget Sound. My legs were tired and my lungs wheezy. All those years of smoking that pipe. The park was quiet for a Sunday. Ahead of me, in the distance, were two figures walking hand in hand. No one has ever squeezed my hand like that.

At the top of the bluff Kristen and Nathan stopped to sit. I wanted to walk towards them but didn't. I opened my bag, paused and braced myself. Raised my bow, nocked the arrow, steadied my aim and pulled back hard until the bow was at full draw and my finger grazed the corner of my mouth. The wind had picked up and my entire body was trembling hard. They were watching a baby eagle in the distance flapping low over the water. It was very hot. I could feel the ticking of my heart. Kristen had rested her head into the crook of his arm. *For I love all of you,* I sang softly. What do I know? I released the bowstring and dropped the bow to my side. Took hold of the arrow and returned it to the quiver.

Trudging along in silence, I turned, and walked in the direction of my home. I had no work to go back to. The sun had hit its sweet spot, saturating the giant madrona tree a brilliant chestnut colour. I followed the light and sat with my bow under the shelter of the tree and tried to gather my thoughts. I'm a weary old man. Tears leaked down my face. I leaned against the smooth solid trunk and unbuttoned my coat, took my last arrow and shoved it into my heart. Love penetrated into me. A rush of stars released from my hands and out the top of my head.

When I opened my eyes Kristen and Nathan were gone, the sun was already down, and Matt Morgan was sitting at my side. My heart leapt at the sight of him. Someone who has been my friend forever. I was dumbstruck and must have looked pale as a ghost.

"That's a beautiful moon tonight, Jacob," he said.

Near to the water, a player was tenderly blowing a saxophone, pulling us into its spell on this warm night. The music and the strangeness of the day and two old friends looking up at the night sky. There was an air of happiness.

LOVE IS THE CROOKED THING

I shivered, and for the life of me I couldn't get warm. It could have been the gusts out here on the quay about to pick me up and drop me back down. Or just the draught of loneliness. I needed a sturdy hand to hold. We're wired that way. For love. I'd been hurrying the length of the Svolvær waterfront, my hair flying and my cheeks tingling. I had to catch myself and try not to feel blue. I've waited all year to make this trip. I didn't know how much time had passed since I began walking this morning. I can usually gauge time, but I was mixed up here with all this light in the north of Norway in June. Lately, everything felt oddly accelerated anyway. One day I was admiring my married friends and I wanted to be grown up, just like them. The next, I was someone with my own empty nest, wishing I could go back, take more risks, seize the day, pull out the stops. Take more lovers.

I slowed when I saw two boys chatting and fishing off the pier. I'd been practising Norwegian place names under my breath, not aloud—I figured I would mangle them. What surprised me was the way I walked right up to them. "Hell-o," I said as I approached. Norwegian accents were intoxicating to me and I was hoping to hear them speak. "Hello," the boys replied, unfazed. After that simple hello, I forgot how cold I was. I wish I could speak the language. One of the boys was holding a fishing pole and the other a bucket of water. The one with the pole was clenching the line as though a fish was going to swim right up to him and take his bait. He should relinquish the line. Let it out more. Fishing is all about confidence.

My dad taught me that. And I remember teaching my son, Ben. "Look," I'd say to Ben, repeating the words Dad said to me.

"It works best when you hold the pole this way." Then I'd demonstrate, holding the pole away from me, lightly inviting the fish to play on the line. Ben would nod his head and go on holding the pole clutched tightly between both hands. At that moment, he made me laugh. Maybe next year he'd be ready for some coaching. There will be no advice from me today.

I peered into the boy's plastic bucket where there were two skinny fish swimming in a half pail of water. The wind had come up again and the boys' fair skin was growing splotchy red. Their focus had shifted to the incoming waves growing larger and lunging against the wharf. They turned their back to the sea and the gusts blew their hair straight up over their heads. They doubled over with laughter.

I was jetlagged, having flown from Vancouver the day before, waiting for Ben to arrive to pick me up. He was working up north for the summer in a small fishing village. The cold was getting the better of me again. I rubbed my hands together. I should have gone back to the hotel for my down jacket, but I kept walking with only a thin hoody and scarf. There's something I love about mornings and blustery air. Yesterday afternoon when I arrived, I'd walked the quay and saw twenty sperm whales swim by. Close up, arching and flipping their tails in single file. Everyone on the quay went silent as the whales passed. I turned to a man beside me and said, "Oh, I don't imagine I could do better than that."

"No big deal," he said. "Just a show for the tourists."

"Well, job well done," I said. We both laughed.

I walked on, trying to imagine seeing Ben after almost a year. I couldn't help feeling a little sad. I loved being a mom. I have a master's degree and I'm head of the math department in my school, but I delighted in the everyday surprises of being a mom. I did what single moms do; I'd get excited about little things. I tried too hard. I brought home a dog when he wanted a dog. I stayed awake into the early hours when he drove off in his friend's old Volkswagen and winced when he showed me his first tattoo. I tried not to have my own plans for him.

After he left for Norway last fall, I burst into tears while explaining my loneliness to my best friend, Nancy. This is what you do when your house becomes quiet. I never said a word to Ben. Then I got down to business keeping busy; riding my bike again and swimming in the mornings at Kits outdoor pool. On an impulse one day, I signed up for swing lessons at the community center. That's where I met Harold McRobbie. They assign you a partner and I got Harold. I'd forgotten how nice it was to have someone to dance with, and Harold made a good partner. Graceful and quick to learn the steps. We had coffee together the morning of our last class. Harold seemed to arrive with high hopes. "Call me," he said.

"I will."

He didn't believe me. He said it three times. I should have called.

It had taken me two days travelling from Vancouver to reach Svolvær, the capital and heart of Lofoten. My guidebook described the town as fairy-tale beautiful. But, to be honest, my first impression had been mixed. For one thing, a dark, threatening, craggy pinnacle, called Svolværgeita, towers above the town. I walked under the shadow of the pillar yesterday and can't say it was what I came here to experience.

"You here to climb the crag?" the hotel concierge asked. "It's on everybody's bucket list."

Climbing the crag wasn't on my bucket list.

"A perfect view of the town's cemetery," he said.

What was that supposed to mean? I was approaching an age when I was uninterested in seeing a place for dead people.

As I paced back and forth in front of the lobby of the hotel making conversation with myself, I noticed my profile in the window and was shocked to see my shoulders hunched. Jesus, who's that old woman? I didn't like turning fifty this year and being single seemed an added insult. I'm active and you'd think that would be enough. Though, as Nancy said, "You can only polish the silver for so long." I stepped back from my reflection, scooped up my chin, carefully retied my scarf the way I noticed the women here in Svolvær were tying theirs. Fuchsia is a good colour next to my fair skin. Fun and jazzy. I straightened my spine and made little fists in the air.

I had arrived in time for the summer solstice. "How will it be in the land of the midnight sun?" I'd asked Ben in an email before I left home.

"Lighter than light, Mom. The sun doesn't set in the summer. The days don't begin or end. You'll see."

Ben didn't ask me to bring him anything from home. I brought gifts anyway. The things he used to like. Coloured roller-ball pens, a jar of chunky peanut butter, his worn copy of *Franny and Zooey*. He could be counted on to quote that book as though Salinger had the final word on the emotional life of a college kid. Ben left the book behind when he left for Norway. It was on his bed with everything to be packed. When I returned from seeing him off at the airport, the book was still there on his bed.

It was exactly a year ago when Ben told me he was leaving. It was a Saturday, I was sitting on the porch, facing the street that morning. I'd been mesmerized by crows dive-bombing out of the sky and onto the earth beak first, foraging for bugs.

"Nice morning, hey?" Ben sat down beside me, bare feet and sweats he'd slept in. He wiped his eyes. He wasn't known for his morning hours.

"Yes, it's an excellent morning," I said. "The sun is shining. The birds are singing. Crows have discovered an abundance of bugs and they're ripping up our garden."

"Mom, I've decided to go to graduate school. I applied ages ago and heard back yesterday."

His words hung in the air as though we'd been having a conversation. Ben was twenty-two. He finished university the year before. He slept until noon. He had a summer job working at a small pub across the city where his friends hung out. He didn't seem to feel excited about anything. I watched as he licked his fingers, dampened tobacco onto a thin rolling paper and deftly rolled the cylinder between fingers and thumbs. He had his father's nose that he'd punctured with a gold ring. The curls of his hair fell black against the paleness of his face, making him seem sad.

"Well, Ben, you're smart as a whip," I said. I had the urge to stand up and scream for joy, but I didn't.

"Smart as a whip. But not happy."

I was sure he was quoting something from *Franny and Zooey*. He dabbed his tongue on the cigarette paper, waited for the glue to hold, squeezed the ends, and lit the thing.

"Why aren't you happy?" I said. "You're young. You've got your whole life ahead of you."

He butted the barely smoked cigarette out on the deck. "That's very nice, Mom. But you know, I feel I'm stuck in a box. I have to move on. Right? I don't know if I can."

"You're so dramatic, Ben. Of course, you can."

"Sometimes this all sounds like a fantasy to me. The future. You know? I want to do something I'm proud of. And I want someone to love me."

"I love you," I said. But I knew what he meant.

He picked the half-smoked cigarette off the step and re-lit it. "You didn't say where."

"Norway. University of Tromsø. Not too far."

Mother and son together on the step. The place where we'd sit and talk. It was nine o'clock on a Saturday morning. I picked up my coffee cup, it was empty. I blinked into the sunlight. He was waiting for my reaction.

"You couldn't find someplace further away?"

"Tasmania, Mom. Tasmania would be further." He gazed down, inhaled the thin butt. I saw the smirk.

Ben was stationed in a hamlet called Melbu for the summer, doing research—lab work for his program at the University of Tromsø - collecting sea samples, measuring water quality. Nancy had asked, "Why Norway?"

"I don't know why Norway exactly. Something to do with the fishery and all of the oil tankers passing through the Norwegian waters." I'd said, making it up. I wanted to say that he was brilliant. Did you see his fourth-year paper? That a number of universities had offered him a generous scholarship. None of that was true. He never applied anywhere else. I worried that Norway was as far away as he could get from home.

Then I heard someone whistle. A good-looking couple was walking towards me. Was it Ben? His arm was stretched around the waist of a very tall well-dressed woman with the most remarkable face. The effect of the sunlight on her eyes was electric. The sea shimmering. And effortless in black pants, jacket and boots. I fingered the edges of my scarf and glanced back at the window. Beige chinos and hiking shoes. I looked like someone's mother.

."There you are," Ben said. He released his grip on the woman. "Mom, so good to see you." Kissed me on both cheeks.

I waited a minute then I folded him in a bear hug. Felt the bones of his back. He was so thin.

"Mom, this is Johanna."

Words fell. He had not mentioned a girlfriend.

"It's cold this morning," she said. She took my hands. Cupped them in her hands. Warm and buzzing, I let her warm me. I'd travelled such a long way.

I looked over her shoulder at Ben. At his face with a goatee I had never seen before. He was blushing. I think he winked at me too. But I wasn't sure. Was that a wink, or a tic? Does he mean we'll talk later? I wanted to say something in Norwegian. *Sa flott.* Hello, and nice to meet you. No, not *sa flott. Sa flott* means great. "*Nydelig.*"

"Hi, I'm Lydia," I said finally. My eyes caught her necklace, a single silver hammered heart. I was suddenly and inexplicably drawn to that heart.

"I love your name, Lydia," she said.

"That's funny, but I never liked my name. I don't dislike it really, but it's my mother's name too."

The heart-shaped necklace was flickering in the sunlight. I pushed at my scarf which had crept up to my chin. My purse was bulging with my book, sunglasses, a map, my travel documents and reading glasses. Thank goodness Nancy had convinced me to pack a dress at the last minute.

"I'm thinking of changing my name."

"Mom, Grandma would freak out," said Ben. He pressed his head up to my ear. "Freak out."

"I don't think she would even know now. Anyway, who doesn't want their own name?"

"Good point," he said, backing up. He picked up my back-pack. "Let's get on the road. We'll be staying in Johanna's family cabin," he said, as the three of us walked towards the car.

"We're working, Johanna and me, collecting samples. We can talk about all that later."

I had pictured him alone at a research station. A small hut with a lab and a bunk bed. Working towards his graduation.

"Do you want the front or the back seat, Mom?"

"Ben, your Mom should go in the front."

"The back," I said, as cheerfully as I could. Hugged my bulging purse to my side and squeezed into the rear of the car.

"We are going to have lots of company. The cottage has been in Johanna's family for years. You're going to love it."

This was only day one. No complaining. I could see Ben in the rearview mirror with a smile plastered on his face. He patted her knee. She's saying his name.

"There's hot running water. No worries."

"It's not far, Lydia. You're sure to see cormorants and sea eagles. Puffins, too. Ben said that's your kind of thing. People on the ferry on our way down said there were whales here yester-day."

"I saw whales yesterday."

"Cool."

We took a ferry, left the archipelago, and followed the fjord to another island. Me trying to take it all in. My son and his girlfriend. The narrow windy road. Farms with sheep grazing. A wooden church alone on a cliff like a lighthouse. The ebbing tide.

"From here to Melbu, you'll see the traditional red fisher-man's cabins, called *rorbu*." Ben maneuvered the steering wheel with one hand, his other hand on the stick shift. Johanna's hand on his hand. I suddenly had a strong urge to ask him to stop the car and let her out. I don't care. We should be laughing and making plans. I should be riding up front.

"There is no industry along here," Ben said in a chirpy voice sounding like a tour guide. "The coastline is still unspoiled. Well, mostly."

"Mostly?" I asked. His shoulder leaned into her shoulder.

"Well, we are here collecting samples. So, maybe not as good as it looks," Johanna said.

"What of the fishery?" I asked. "Sounds like Norway has the same worries we have back home."

"Fishery's almost done, Mom. Norway is wealthy with oil now."

"Were you raised here, Johanna?" I asked. "In the north? It's beautiful."

"My family is from Tromsø. We've summered up here since I was a child. Grandfather built the cottage himself." Her English was perfect. Her sentences rose up at the end, like a musical note.

"I'm looking forward to seeing it." I reached for a note at the end of my sentence. Trying to hold it together. What if he marries her? He will never come home.

"I have to warn you. Everyone goes a little crazy in summer in the north of Norway, after the long cold dark winter." She drew a circle with her finger in front of her ear. "As soon as the light gets bright we live outdoors. People will drop in uninvited. No one wants to waste one minute. It's fun, really."

When Ben was in middle school, we would have pizza night on Friday nights. Just the two of us. After the delivery guy left, he'd put a sign on the front door, Keep Out. It was a joke, intended for his friends. But there weren't many friends. That was a misstep on my part. I should have pushed him to be more social. I couldn't imagine him in a small town with people coming over uninvited.

We pulled into a narrow lane and drove towards a wooden, square-logged cottage. Inside the summerhouse were lace curtains, pine walls, oil lamps, an enormous stone fireplace, and carved wooden benches covered in animal hide. Nothing changed in fifty years.

Johanna showed me to my room. I followed her to the back of the cottage. We ducked our heads under the low log doorway and entered the bedroom.

"This is my favourite room," she said, crossing to the closet to retrieve a knit blanket. "You might need this. It's been cold at night." She smoothed the bedding, fluffed the pillows. The heart on her neck swayed. "*Takk*," I said, and lowered my pack onto the plank floor.

"Everything is perfect," I said. "Let's take a walk."

"You must be tired. No?"

"I'm fine, really."

"Just like Ben. Go, go, go. I think Canadians are like Norwegian people."

We took a footpath following the coastline. Ben in the middle, holding both our hands. Just like family. The sun was warmer. After a while, we came to an outcropping with views down into the valley, painted houses in all colours, the long ribbon of fjord flowing out to the Norwegian Sea.

"All of it looks blue, doesn't it, Mom?"

"You're right about that," I said. The grasses, the rocky shoreline, the craggy summit, the light off the water, even the small birds flitting in the scrub.

"Probably caused by all this light north of the Arctic Circle," he said. "I think the spectrum changes. Or how we see it changes."

After the walk, Johanna and Ben made dinner. I offered to help, but they wouldn't have it, so I went to my room, pulled the knit blanket up to my shoulders, and fell asleep. When I heard a knock on the bedroom door I had been dreaming of flying. I had wings and tail feathers. I was a bald eagle soaring on thermals, covering long distances above trees and a great winding river. Fields covered in crops. Herds of wild reindeer running through their summer pastures.

"Dinner's ready, Lydia." That voice like musical notes.

After dinner, we sat on the carpet in front of the fire and played cribbage. The air was cool in the cottage. Johanna gave me a wool sweater and a pair of knitted socks. Ben sprawled on the floor beside Johanna. Her woollen feet rested on his woollen feet. She was in love with him.

"How's Grandpa?" Ben asked.

"He's okay. You know Grandpa. He just keeps going. Sort of."

"And Grandma?" he asked, shuffling the cards.

"Well, she doesn't say much now. She pushes me or pokes my arm. She shows me what she wants me to do."

"It's good they have you."

"I suppose," I said, leaning in to cut the deck, turning up a jack.

I realized the boy in his man's face. Such a long time ago. And no time at all.

I woke up early. It was 4 a.m. and the sky was twilight, layered in orange. I was happy for the wool sweater, built a fire, settled down at the hearth, leaned into the light and read my book.

We ate breakfast and Johanna and Ben left for work. After they were gone, I took a walk, read, napped. Simple things I would have scoffed at back at home. Our days went like that. Settling into a rhythm. Long with the light.

In the mornings, Ben and Johanna collected their samples from the sediment, looking for oil residues that they will later measure in the lab at the university. In the afternoons we would walk, kayak, and swim.

People visited practically every evening. We'd make a fire after dinner, talk, play games, make plans.

On the afternoon of my last day, the three of us walked to the boathouse, took out the kayaks and hauled them into the water for a final outing.

Johanna was strong with a terrific cadence and was well in the lead. Maybe it was a Norwegian thing. For a while, Ben and I hung back, paddled beside each other. I was taking one last look at the remote shoreline at the fishermen's cabins with their drying racks. Skerries and little bays. The puffins grunting like pigs. There was a mother duck with ducklings swimming in a line behind our boats. Ben and I made eye contact.

"I find myself counting them all the time," he said. "Afraid by the end of summer some of them won't have made it."

"They're not out of harm's way?"

"Well, they aren't. Half of them won't make it."

I pointed to one duckling that lagged behind all the others. The mother circled back and bobbed in place until the little one swam onto her back. Then they took off in their procession again.

"Don't say anything, Mom. I know what you're thinking."

"What?"

"That the mother will keep them safe."

"I wasn't thinking that at all. I was thinking that little duckling can't swim on its mother's back forever."

Ben rolled his eyes. "Oh, love is the crooked thing."

"Yeats," I said.

"Yup."

It was getting late. I didn't need to look at my watch. I could tell by the way the wind had picked up that it was mid-afternoon. Waves started rising and coming in fast. We hurried to catch up to Johanna. Water showered over the bow. Swells were growing fierce. My eyes watered. I paddled harder.

When we came around the bend there was her kayak lying on its side bobbing like a cork in the waves.

"Johanna!" hollered Ben.

I rammed my knees into the rim of the cockpit. Pulled into the wind with all my might.

"Johanna!" No response.

We paddled up on either side of the lilting kayak. Johanna was flopped on her side crumpled like a fallen branch. Her lips were blue. Her hands curled tight onto the paddle half submerged. Water poured into the tipped boat.

I steadied the kayak while Ben rolled it upright. "Hey!" he yelled.

Knowing and not knowing what to do, I reached for her hands and rubbed vigorously while Ben pulled her upright. Her chest wheezed and churned. Her cheeks returned to normal co-lour. Unbelievably, she took hold of her paddle and started to move.

"I'm okay. Let's take it slow," she said.

Ben met my gaze. I couldn't catch my own breath.

"I don't know," he said. "I'll tow you back."

"I can do it myself," she said.

We took it slow on the way back and pulled our kayaks out of the water.

"Let's go for a swim," said Johanna, shoving her paddle inside his kayak.

"Why swim when we had a catastrophe?" I was shaken and could barely stand up on my wet, wobbly legs. "Maybe we should go to a doctor."

"No. Definitely not. We are alive, Lydia, better to move."

I stared into those green eyes. I can't explain. Then the two of them were gone. Racing each other to the end of the dock. They stripped off their clothes and cannonballed into the icy cold sea.

I watched, bewildered. What was I doing here? Then something switched in me. I had to go, too. Jump into the freezing water. Before I die. Something a little terrifying. The next thing I knew, I was standing at the end of the wharf peeling off my clothes. Then I leapt feet first into the stinging cold water of the fjord. When I surfaced, I couldn't speak. I paddled in a circle. I reached with my toes searching for the bottom. There was no bottom. My teeth chattered. I was too skinny with no fat to keep me warm. I suddenly imagined Harold McRobbie with his mouth swirling around my small frozen breasts. Like it was spring, and I was young. What happens to the heart? Johanna and Ben were racing each other, swimming out to sea. Love is a crooked thing.

After the swim, we climbed the hill back to the *hytte*. It was my final night in Melbu. We had dinner to prepare before the guests arrived.

Ben and Johanna had invited Lisbeth and Svein from next door, a fellow named Anders, I hadn't met yet, and Leif and Kristen, two students also working for the summer at the marine sciences station.

"They will stay for midnight dessert and the bonfire," said Johanna. "This is traditional for midsummer, Lydia. Soon you will be gone. You mustn't worry about me."

I wore the printed summer dress I'd brought and lipstick to match. No scarf and no chinos. While I was drying my hair, Johanna opened the bathroom door. As I stood there facing the mirror, she lifted my hair and placed her heart necklace around my neck and fastened the clasp. "This is for you. Life is fragile," she said. Then she was gone.

We prepared crackers and dip, small salted fish, and set mutton and potatoes to roast on the outdoor grill.

Anders arrived first. Rang the doorbell and let himself in. With long strides like a dancer he came towards me, leaned within inches of my face. "Pleased to meet you, Ben's mother." He was tall with long unruly hair. Like he didn't care at all about his appearance. Unspeakably handsome. His voice was too loud. There was no space between our faces. His arm was on my shoulder as if we knew each other. I shrank from his hold. Other guests were arriving.

Anders offered the plate of salted cod. "Aren't you hungry, Ben's mom?" His eyes were intense. Black as the night. In this place of no night. There was somewhere a shudder in me I could not stop. No one touches me now. Burrow into his shoulder. Undress. How would it feel to be taken to bed?

I moved to the grill. "Should we turn this thing over?" I called to Ben.

When Ben rose to his feet, I could see all over again that he was handsome, thinner, and very cool in red shorts and a teal blue shirt. Norway had unlocked a style in him. His lips curled as he smiled. I had a flash of his dad, twenty-five years ago, lingering in the doorway after class, the night we met. The night we'd stayed awake and talked and talked that turned into three nights. The night Ben was conceived. Then he was gone. Back home to North Carolina. I never heard from him again.

"I don't know," Ben said, poking at the meat with a fork.

"It's probably close to being done. I don't think you can hurt it."

"Anders thinks you're hot, Mom."

"What! I'm twice his age. And your mother." I said and shrugged my shoulders and my longing.

"Yeah, I know. But people don't look at you and see a mother. I was just noticing. That's all."

There was silence. I wanted to confide in him. That youth won't last. That it will be suddenly and conspicuously gone.

"You're still smoking," I said instead.

"I'm trying to quit," he mumbled, waving his cigarette over the grill.

"You don't have to do it for me," I said, catching his eye.

"I know, Mom." He gently bumped me with his shoulder. "That was a love bump." Then walked away, back to his guests.

We sat outside on plastic chairs around the fire pit and ate dinner. Beer and wine were floating in a big tin bucket of water and ice. I never saw so much drinking in my life. Anders kept leaping out of his chair to demonstrate something. How windy it was in the mountains on his hiking trip. How the suspension bridge shook as he crossed over. Everyone was listening. Laughing. We never mentioned our afternoon in the kayaks.

"*Forsiktig*," said Kristen. "Maybe it was too windy to cross."

"There is always sign in Norway. Walk this way. Don't walk that way," said Leif. "You should pay attention."

"I wiggled my fingers and toes as I walked, trying to keep them from going numb. My nose is cold. My hands are cold. The top of my head is cold. I'm trying not to look down." Anders cavorted back and forth in front of the fire.

I began shaking with the memory of Johanna gone cold only hours ago.

"After a while, clouds descend, and the temperature drops suddenly. I pull on my jacket. What visibility we had earlier is fast disappearing. I am uncertain about whether to go forward or back. I pull my plastic poncho. This thing is useless." He heaves a weightless imaginary poncho to the ground. "You're going to freeze, Anders."

"But it is always this way on Saltfjellet. Why you have not brought warm jacket?" shouted Svein.

The dancer turned in a clumsy pirouette. "It is a mystery to me too, Svein. I plod on. When I reach the top, remarkably, I am in sunlight. I look down at my soaked shoes. My wet socks. My fingers are blue. I see only blue." He concludes the performance, wrapping his hands around his chest, shaking with cold.

What were we doing swimming after the kayaking accident?

"The blue is the blue of the Wolf Man," Johanna said, shaking her head, laughing. "He is a creature, half man, half wild animal. He lives in the mountains," she explained, glancing over at me. "He watches over the hikers. It's true, Anders. Yes? Saltfjellet didn't get you today."

Did he watch over Johanna, I wonder? Is she saying that?

"He isn't finished," Lisbeth said. "What did you do?" But Anders had finished. He was taking a beer from the ice bucket. Everyone had returned to eating.

"I have a drink, of course," he said laughing and took a bow. He was like a child bursting for acceptance. Desire rose in me again. I finished my dinner. He had barely touched his plate.

Ben and Johanna took the dishes to the kitchen, Anders pulled out a joint. He hadn't taken his eyes off me. I'm not imagining. He swirled the fat joint in front of his long nose, sniffing the length of it, as though he was sniffing a cigar. Then he took out a lighter and went into the cottage with Ben and Johanna.

I sat beside Lisbeth and Svein for a while. They were pleasant to talk to. No one seemed to mind Anders.

It was almost midnight when Ben and Johanna came outside with the coffee. The music was louder. Voices clattered the way they do when people were drinking.

"Don't worry. Everything doesn't have to be so perfect." That was Ben. Through the open doorway, I saw them bent over, scraping a cake off the floor and back onto a plate.

"I just want everything to be nice for your mom."

"It is nice. She doesn't expect everything to be perfect."

I should not have witnessed this incident with the smashed cake on the floor. I turned around and walked back to the bench outside.

When they came out Johanna was carrying the cake topped with whipped cream, blueberries and strawberries. The cake was lop-sided. Some of the berries crushed.

"This is Norwegian midsummer cake, for a celebration. We are celebrating Ben's mom visiting from Canada."

"*Vakkert.*" I said. There was a lump rising in my throat. I was celebrating that Johanna was alive. *You could be my daughter-in-law.*

"When did you make this?"

"Last night when you were all sleeping."

No one mentioned the accident with the cake.

Ben and Johanna added wood to the fire until it was the size of a bonfire. They were turned to each other, grinning like children. We ate the cake and sang songs in Norwegian. I had no idea what I was singing. Then we drank coffees and sipped something like schnapps. The sky was bright, layers of citrus light that didn't settle into twilight at all. It was well after midnight when I decided to go to bed. Ben and Johanna were dozing on the bench outside. I found a fur blanket and draped it over them. "Goodnight," I whispered and kissed each forehead.

"Sit with me, Ben's mom." Anders' voice was coming from the front door. His face lit by the half shadow of twilight.

"Lydia," I said. "It's late."

"Not too late for you."

He pulled a flask from his jacket pocket. "Norwegian whisky. *Akevitt.* You have to try."

He handed the flask to me. I took a swig and let it roll around in all the corners of my mouth. Warmth flooded into the top of my head until I felt a little dizzy.

"You are pretty. Yes." He leaned into me.

"How old are you?" I asked.

"I'm twenty-eight. An old man now." He laughed, taking another swig from the flask. Handed the flask to me.

"Do you have a lover?"

"I'm fifty. This year."

"That's good."

"No, it's not good."

"Why do you think like this? You need a lover." He leaned into my face and kissed me. I didn't resist. We leaned into the threshold against the door. He was tender. I was remembering.

"I am a mother. Ben's mother."

He threw back his head laughing. "Yes," he said. "I have not forgotten." Handed me the flask again. "Everyone has a chance to be happy. No? Even the mother."

"Yes, they do. Now it is time to say goodnight. I depart tomorrow." I touched his forehead with my forehead, his shoulder.

"One more for the journey." He handed me the flask. I drank again.

"*Godnatt*, Lydia. Safe home." Then he left. Simply and swiftly gone.

I walked clumsily to my room at the back of the cottage. There was light coming in through the small windows, half illuminating the walls, the doorway with its low beam, where I ducked my head. I crawled into bed. The spicy bittersweet licorice taste of

Akevitt teasing me. Closed my eyes. The last remaining wild reindeer were running through their summer pastures. I was running with them. The light was blinding.

The next morning, I readied myself for the trip home. Johanna gave me a hug and handed me a package of food.

"Just some things to keep you from starving," she said. "Ben's going to take you back to Svolvær. You could probably use some mother–son time."

"Do you mind taking it back?" Ben asked once we were on the way. His copy of *Franny and Zooey* on the floor of the car. "I don't think anybody was happy in the end."

I picked up the book, rolled down the window, and heaved the book out in the direction of the sea. "Best not to waste one minute on it."

"Just like that, Mom?"

"Just like that."

Nancy met me at the airport, buzzing to hear all about my trip. The air was cold in Vancouver. Tips of the leaves already changing colour. In Tromsø, the sky will soon be dark. Mushrooms will be ready for foraging. The lingonberries have all been picked. The cod, what's left of them, will be making their way to the coast to spawn.

The next day I called Harold McRobbie. It seems he swims in the mornings at Kits pool, too. Harold and I dove in, swam the length of the pool, stroke by stroke, 137 metres alongside English Bay. The sun's rays warming the cool air. The trilling wrens in the blackberry thicket. Chestnut leaves turning. Straight into autumn.

II
Bend to Love

In a dark time, the eye begins to see.

—Theodore Roethke

LOST LAKE

Man

It's early morning. Thick with dark and quiet, cool for September even here in the foothills. I'm on my bike, my headlamp illuminating the valley trail. The sky bright with stars. Crows fill these woods in the evening with their din and commotion, but not now. I hear only my tires striking the dirt of the trail, sending pebbles scrambling. This is the track I take every day. I come to these woods to still my mind. Who am I? This question never leaves me. Soon this route will be impassable with snow. But not yet. This morning I am a wolf. I'm not a howling wolf. I'm zigzagging through the trees, watching.

I know my territory. I have defined my boundary over the past twenty years; between the lake and the ridge where the terrain gets steep and dense with fir trees, I am free to pass.

After an hour or so the trail winds low, dropping to the path around the lake. Soon there will be tourists, runners with dogs. But no one at this hour. People think that I want to be alone. It's not so. I want more than anything to live with others. I dream of my mother. Her brown eyes, her warm hands, her voice when she sang me to sleep. I wish I had aunts, sisters and brothers. I keep riding, remembering my old man with his snarling rage. I never forget that he left me here to die.

I am leaning into my bike, grazing fir branches, breathing the underside of leaves, when I see a boy not more than six metres ahead of me. The sun leaks first light over the treetops, though it is mostly dark in the woods. He is only the outline of an image. As I ride nearer, I see eyes dark as raven's eyes looking into the distance, his hands swinging wildly holding something I cannot see. Is he playing with a make-believe toy? A plastic airplane perhaps? Or trying to throw a knife?

I slow my bike. His dark eyes slip under my skin. The way his feet turn in when he walks. And pitifully thin. He looks like a kid from that story *Hansel and Gretel* left alone in the forest.

No shoes, short-sleeved shirt, no hat. Even now, the autumn sun will soon be scorching. What is he doing here all alone? Where is his mother? His father? As we come close to each other he drops his arms to his side and his eyes to the ground. He keeps walking as if he is unafraid. As if he's been here before and knows the way. I don't know why but I don't stop for the boy.

Boy

I didn't sleep last night. I lay down between two big trees on some moss and branches. My belly was empty. I wanted honey on some bread and a cup of milk. The dark got darker. The moss under me got cold and wet. I got up to pee, walked into thick boughs I couldn't see, and peed on myself. The trees were whispering. A wolf was howling. Then another and another. Maybe wolves will eat me. Curled into a ball trying to get warm. I looked out at the darkness of the lake when it suddenly got quiet. "Sing to me, Mom." She tucked me in. "Wait, I'm thirsty," I said. She gave me a glass of warm milk. The big moon came out like a lamp. I closed my eyes and listened to her sing of children lost in the woods. All night they had to huddle to stay warm. Then in the daytime they walked and walked until at last they came to a cottage.

As soon as the sun came up, I walked and walked. I've walked around this lake three times remembering everything about my home before my mom died. I could go in the other direction. It's not a big lake, this lake. I wonder where is the swimming beach? This is a no-good lake. And my dad is gone.

"We'll do a little fishing. Then we'll stop for a picnic. That'll be nice. There's sandwiches we packed and what about those peaches?"

We were just walking and talking and suddenly he wasn't there. Then I heard his truck leaving. Way far in the distance. I chased after the noise. But we'd parked so far away and walked through the forest. And I don't know where.

"That's not nice," I yelled. I am like a drum, yelling. Then all I could hear was wind bending the treetops. He took the fishing poles and my runners. He didn't say anything. He was just gone.

Man

I have been riding the trails around Lost Lake since I was a boy. I'm thirty this year. I have nowhere else to go. It's good. Local people know me, but they keep their distance. They say hello, the way you would say hello to a stranger. I know this doesn't make sense for a lonely man, but I go out early, before the walkers and other cyclists arrive. Riding into the yellow slant light of morning and the scent of fir and cedar, stirring up dust and loose scree. Sinking into a rhythm. I'm not thinking. I'm emptying.

During the week, I teach mountain bike skills to the kids in town. Last summer, boys fifteen to seventeen years. All eager daredevils. This summer I've got boys seven to nine. Simple stuff, easy technical skills—going over rocks, roots, small logs. Maneuvering on single track. How to pop a wheelie. They're different than the older boys. Quieter, more serious, their eyes set on the trail. You can hear the sounds of the forest, the *tap tap tap* of a woodpecker, crows snatching the litter, fighting over scraps of food. I have to remind myself to look back, keep an eye on each kid, make sure no one is falling behind.

Of course, I try to keep them within their skill level. I'm not trying to frighten anyone. But this kid, Adam, couldn't loosen up and relax on his bike. His arms always moving, the crazy way one of his knees wouldn't track straight, the way he would climb, flinging his bike from side to side trying to hold his balance. Always screaming, "I don't know what gear I am in!"

"Mountain biking isn't for everyone," I suggested to his parents. "Adam's a good swimmer. That might be his thing." But Adam was the one that kept coming back. Like a fox in a clearing.

Always looking at me for something.

All the water birds you expect to see on ordinary lakes—herons, wrens, terns, bitterns—I have never seen here. There might be a hawk overhead, circling. And soon tiny toads will make a pilgrimage from lake to land, starting their amphibian life. They cross all the trails and you have to watch for them. Every day of their journey, half of them will die, flattened by cyclists and walkers. They will shrivel up and be swallowed back into the earth.

Boy

You'd think there'd be some berries like in our field at home. Mom and me would be picking blackberries. She was a good picker. I always got my baseball cap full. But there were so many prickly bushes. Picking blackberries is hard work. I'm so hungry. Mom would have packed sandwiches and a blanket for a picnic at a lake with a sandy beach for swimming. After, when I would be cold, she would wrap me in the blanket, and I'd put my head on her lap.

Man

The grass is bent with dew and my tires are slipping. My hands are gripping my bike when they should be loose. The lake when I reach it is flat and gloomy. How dark this lake can be. Mist hovers, pushed down by the cold air at night. The sun is quickly beginning to warm the air and the haze starts to lift. Drifting on currents that can't be seen but you know are there. Up the valley, mysterious and beautiful, like maybe there is a heaven. And Mom is there. I watch unable to turn away. Then I am distraught by the vanishing. Like Mom leaving again without saying good-bye. I zip my jacket all the way up my neck and carry on.

Boy

The sun is hot. My eye's twitching. The ground is moving and I'm kind of dizzy. I sit down. Look at those tiny toads, hundreds of them. Little as my thumb. Tom Thumb toads. I take my knife out of my pocket and lay it on the ground. The toads crawl over the blade like it's a hill and keep on going without a sound. I could stick my blade in them and squish them dead. But you have to pay for what you do. God knows all these things. I put my knife away. I have to keep walking. I have to make it to my home.

Man

I spot a black bear traversing the ridge up out of the valley. His body lumbering slow. I'm shocked by how startled and defenseless I become. Like a boy wanting to hide, even though it's bear season and bears are common here. He looks thin and hungry, the bones of his shoulders protruding. He'll be coming low looking for berries. I slam on my brakes waiting for him to pass.

"Bear is your animal guide," Mom would tell me at night when I was small and couldn't fall asleep. "I don't know what you mean," I'd say. Mom had all kinds of superstitions.

"Your protector, Joe." She'd kiss me and lie with me until I drifted off. The hairs on my arms and neck were tingling. Something was passing through the woods right now, like a ghost. I walked for a while then got back on my bike and took the trail down to the lake.

Boy

What's that huffing and puffing? Yuk. Smells like an old wet blanket. Holy moly, there's a black bear. He's massive. He's so close. I bet he's looking for his breakfast. I'm not afraid of Bear. Mom said Bear is my protector. I can tell all of my worries to Bear. Then I won't be afraid of shadows and scary people and bad things happening. Can you help me, Bear? I'm all alone. And I don't know where is my home. My dad left me in the forest yesterday. We were supposed to go fishing at this lake. Were we going to go fishing on that dock? I hope not. The last time I was on a dock we were on our way home from the city last winter. I was holding Mom in a tin box. Dad said we were going to spread her ashes. "What is this spreading ashes, Dad?" Dad can be a chatterbox, all day, on and on.

But when you want to know something, he goes quiet.

"You pour them into the ocean. Or among the trees. Back into nature where we came from, son."

We stopped in a town on the way home. Not our town. Dad drove the truck out onto a long wharf I'd never seen before. To the very end. "Get out, boy." I couldn't budge. But he said it again. When Dad says things twice, he means business.

I got out carrying Mom. I had to hold the box tight with both hands and use all my muscles. We opened the box. The waves were crashing big and it was windy and started raining. Dad took a handful and leaned over the side of the dock and dropped her in the water. Then I put my hand in. I couldn't loosen my fist of ashes. Water splashed my face. I aimed for the end of the dock throwing my handful of Mom into the waves. Some of Mom went in the water and some the wind pushed back onto me, onto my face. I swallowed some of Mom. She's in my belly.

Bear keeps walking like he doesn't even see me. One day I will be a man. I will be strong. I will be like Bear. I have to keep walking. I hate my dad. My feet are sore. I need my runners. My throat feels like a dust storm. I'm not crying. I'm just looking and thinking about flapping my wings and taking off into the sky world.

Man

If you were expecting motorboats, water skiing, and children's laughter you will be disappointed. Lost Lake is not that kind of lake. It's surrounded by Douglas firs, western cedar, ponderosa pines. The mountains rising purple and clear of snow now. Some mornings I see people fishing at the dock. Spinning a fly rod. Looking content. It's a catch and release lake. Stocked with Dolly Varden, rainbow trout, and cutthroat. I have no stomach for fishing though. Or standing on that dock.

Boy

If I had my bike I could get outta here. I'm the fastest boy in my grade. On sports day I won two blue ribbons for distance and obstacle course. Obstacle was super easy, just had to go around a bunch of plastic cones. Then Dad took my ribbons away. Said I hadn't earned them fair and square. Like I was just doing the thing I do every day. I had to make our dinner and clean up every night for a week to get my ribbons back. So, I did. Then he was asleep on the couch and wouldn't wake up. I could pop a wheelie on these rocks. Watch me, mean old man. I'll get my ribbons back. I'll run right over you.

Man

I don't have any children. I don't know why but I'm still thinking about that boy. It's as if he's waiting for me. Like he walked right into my insides. You never know what they're thinking. I lived for a while with a foster family until I was eighteen. There were five other boys. Karen, the mom wanted me to leave town for university. "You're smarter than the other boys."

"How can you be sure?" I asked so many times.

"Well, I just know, Joe."

So, I went. But I couldn't do it. Skipped classes. Didn't hand in my work. It wasn't for me. I finally came back to the lake and these woods. Trees twenty and twenty feet tall as my mom would say. No matter how many times I came to this earthy smell of soil, moss, and lichen, this old man's beard, the sting of pine needles flicking my face, it rocks my sorrow.

A grouse fluttered, surprised by the suddenness of my bike. I climbed the switchbacks rutted by snowmelt until I hit my stride. Seeing things. The sun's been cresting the mountain later and later. I didn't sleep well last night and woke early, tears pooled on my pillow. I had been trying to reach a small hand. A child's hand. Not this child walking alone around the lake this morning. I don't know who.

Boy

Tap tap tap. That's a woodpecker. I know a woodpecker sound. I bet he's hungry. Maybe he's looking for his home. There's a hawk over my head. I wish I had my plane. I could take off and fly. I would be free. I would fly over these trees. I would be big as the sky and go anywhere I want to go. I feel for my knife in my pocket. The knife Grandpa gave me. I wish I never see my dad again. He wouldn't do that if Mom were here.

Man

If that boy were taller or older, I would think him a homeless person. The way he moved with an invisible bubble around him. And passed by. It's only the first day of autumn. There's the lake and the woods flush with salmon berries. And mushrooms, enough to survive I suppose.

Boy

I'm hollering for my mom. Who wants my mean old dad anyway? There are no people at this lake. Where are the people? My legs are wobbly, but I can't stop walking. I'm looking for the sandy part. When I get to the sandy part, I'm going to make a giant SOS so they can find me.

Man

But children are like secrets, aren't they? We're not supposed to stop and pry if they're not ours. There is a kind of do-not-touch space about them. I don't think he's abandoned. This was just a dirty kid walking all alone. On those little legs. Might be lost. Might be scared. Wind whispering in the tall trees might be frightening.

Boy

I bet the police were searching for me. But who's going to let them know? It's summer holidays. My teacher doesn't know I'm missing. My grade three teacher doesn't even know me yet. My friends Harvey and Tom will be looking for me. Pretty sure about that. If I made a fire, they will see my smoke. Then they will know where I am.

Man

I have the urge to call out his name. But by then I've long passed by. And there is no name. Only the wind rustling branches. Could I give him a name? Shout a made-up name as I ride? Yell, "No Name."

I ride wildly, my bike flying over gravel, tree stump, and rock face. Agile and quick. I have learned a lot from riding. Learned not to be afraid riding alone through the dark woods. I used to be scared riding by myself and rode as fast as I could to get through the dark parts. I could have turned pro a few years ago, but I lacked confidence to go up against the other boys. It's too late now for a man my age. So, I ride for the enjoyment of it. On the lake trails I know by heart. Every turn and undulation. Every root and rock.

I ride faster. The opposite way around the lake. Travelling back days, years, distance. Memories loosening like scree. Past my body's edge. The trees circling, the lake growing darker. All of nature leaning in feverishly. My mind's buzzing. I need to see that boy again.

Boy

I got rocks in my pocket. I picked up all kinds of stones before it got dark last night. I should be dropping them. I gotta be smart. Smarter than my dad. Hansel and Gretel smart. I could put my dad in that oven. It's like snowing. Big puffy white balls. Swooshing off those bushes and sticking on me. If I can make the puffy balls stick on the ground, then the police will find me. They will get my dad and put him in jail.

Man

I didn't mean to, but I'd closed my eyes. I rode away from the light. Spooked like a lone wolf. Afraid of stopping. Afraid of seeing the dark eyes, the uncombed hair, the skinny legs, the dirty feet. I flew over my handlebars. My arms were swinging wildly trying to brace my fall. Taking off and landing. Dirt and mud under my skin. Until there was nowhere more to go than the earth. And a child's small hand, in my hand.

Boy

Skipping stones. My eyes fixed on the water. Pleased with the big ripples I was making. Stumbling and falling. Dragging me down this cliff. Grabbing branches. Branches breaking. Can't stop. Little birds were chirping like they don't even care. Jeepers, there was a bear across the lake. I yelled at everything. Like pounding a drum. At the lake, trees, rocks, at the sky. At Bear. Get me outta here. Until I landed on the earth. Unmoving.

Man

I rode everyday into the light where cottonwood seeds were lifting and spinning on currents I could not see but knew were there. Trying to ride past my history. Until my body travelled the dark path back to you. Lost child by the lake. My hand in your hand. I hesitated for a moment. "Hello. What are you doing out here all alone? I saw you walking." But the little boy didn't want to talk about that. He had something in his other hand. It wasn't a toy plane but a pocketknife with a deer antler handle the size of his hand and a brass guard. The kind of knife that would be passed down. He threw the knife deftly into the bark of a tree. Stabbing the tree. Hollering, "I don't care if he ever comes back." Like I wasn't even there. A dog was barking. People were walking around the lake now. "I don't care either," I said. He looked at me then. I hardly dared to know.

No Ordinary Light

I haven't seen my twin sister in thirty years. I just got off the phone from our friend Paula. "I'm sorry. It leaves such a hole," she said. The dog was barking at the birds in the yard and I could barely hear what she was saying. "I guess you'll be going to Amsterdam. I'll send a card. Do you have the address?"

"No, not right here," I said. My voice was croaky like there was cotton wool down there.

"Let me know how it goes."

"Yes," I said. "Right." How it goes. My sister was dying. It could only go one way.

I'd called Dad. "That's good you're going, son," he said. "It's been a long time." I had half a mind to say something more. We'd both let her down. It was too late. He was in a senior's home with a bad heart and legs the size of watermelons. He couldn't make it to the bathroom on his own. Mom was six months gone. Before she died, she told me her greatest disappointment was not taking Martha in when she came home after university. I didn't know. "Your father told her it was time to make her own way. I tried to talk him out of it, but he was having none of that. She had a girlfriend, Ron. It wasn't on."

At the time, I had a flat on Bathurst Street. When Martha arrived back in Toronto, she asked to crash at my place until she got on her feet. I said yes. She needed money too. I never learned if she had a partner or if she was running away from something. And I had no idea Dad had said she couldn't stay at home. She bunked on the couch, stayed up late watching television, and slept in. She never looked for work and barely changed out of her bathrobe.

One day, I sat on the couch with her, waited for the news to end, and told her she had to go.

"You need a push. Find your old friends. Get a job, an apartment, a life going." She didn't say a thing. She left the next day while I was at work. I heard she went to Amsterdam, eventually found a job, and stayed. I tried for a while to reach her. I wrote letters and asked her friend Paula to pass them on. I had conversations with Paula. She was brisk and sort of threw it back at me. "You're family. You let her down." Martha never spoke to me again.

I didn't know Martha was gay until our last year of university. We were in Vancouver and away from our parents back in Toronto. She was planning to be in the Pride Parade and had asked me to come. So, I did. I stood alone in the crowd as rainbow-coloured floats passed by with guys in G-strings and cowboy hats dancing to "If I Could Turn Back Time." There was a drag queen with ice cream cones glued to his breasts screeching with glee and people with flags and feather boas blowing kisses and handing out glittering beads. The guy beside me was crying. "Is this your first Pride?" he asked. It was like a foreign land to me. I was horrified that someone I knew might see me. When Martha rode by under a *Dykes on Bikes* banner, I waved and laughed nervously. I wish now that I'd been bolder. Shouted out, "Hey, Sis!" Her thick dark curls had been chopped off. Her hair was dyed pink. She looked beautiful.

Six months later, I was back in Toronto and had started my architecture internship at Arthur Simons when I received a phone call. "I'm thinking of coming home too. Just thinking about it."

I was always walking on eggshells with Martha. She was loud and talkative, and she could chop you to your knees with a word. But she was charming, and people liked her. When we had a disagreement, I kept my thoughts to myself. That's how we stayed close. Until I asked her to leave.

I can't sleep. I lay in bed counting out the years on my fingers. Thirty years seemed impossible. It's crazy, but only a month ago I'd taped a crinkled black and white photograph onto the corner of my desk. It was dated 1966. One year after we were born. We were sitting together on a blanket in a field somewhere. Martha was posing for the camera and had the viewer's attention. I was reaching for the cracker Dad had in his hand. The sun was casting a narrow light across his face. Our faces, Martha's and mine, were in shadow.

I didn't sleep on the flight to Amsterdam. My daughter Annie, in her third year at U of T, asked to come. I was happy to have her with me.

"What happened between you and Martha, Dad?"

"I don't know. Over time, I plastered it over. It's the Dutch in me."

"You talk to me. We have difficult conversations."

"I was young then. I didn't know how to fix it. And after a while it was like nothing had happened. And anyway, you force me to talk. It's not my nature."

"You sound like Grandpa. You don't say sorry."

Then I watched films and listened to music. I can be a stupid guy. We hauled our bags up three flights of steep stairs where I'd rented an apartment around the corner from the Herengracht canal. Annie tapped on the window of a small café after the taxi dropped us.

"Let's eat here, Dad."

I looked through the window into the darkness of one of the oldest cafés in Amsterdam.

"You know, maybe I was here before."

"Perfect then."

So, we had dinner at a corner window in the De Reiger Café. Faced the canal, watched people as they rushed by on bicycles on their way home from work. One man rode by gripping a bottle of milk with one hand and steering with the other.

"Let's rent bikes, tomorrow Dad," Annie said. She tapped the base of her half-finished glass of wine. A little flick, like Martha might do.

"There is no way in hell I could balance a heavy Dutch bike with one hand."

"You don't have to ride with one hand. It's for fun."

"We're here for Martha."

"Right, of course."

My bedroom faced the street. It was quiet. Annie was on her phone. I lay dozing and tried to remember my sister. It was like rooting through a shoebox of old photos. I could see us during the summer holidays at the cottage in our leaky rowboat. I rowed and Martha bailed. We were in the doorway of the house on Church Street. I was wearing my Scout uniform and Martha her Girl Guide tunic. She had an arm's length of badges. I had three. In every photograph of us, Martha's eyes were focused off into the distance. Not at the camera. Like she was going somewhere.

I looked out the window as people hurried by on bicycles. Morning light came over the rounded rooftops and facades across the street. In seconds the light grew with such force that I couldn't see anything of the building tops. There was a woman wearing a red knit scarf and a short little jacket. Slim and dark-haired, she whizzed by on an upright bike. I rose and watched her until she disappeared, deftly steering her bicycle around the corner. For about a year after Martha left my apartment, I would see her everywhere. Once, leaving the bank, there was a flash of a woman's face with Martha's hair, those dark almond eyes. Wearing a black turtleneck sweater as Martha would do. I approached her, stopped in front of her I was so certain, before swiftly pulling myself to the side.

Some people say sorry easily. It's true what Annie said. In our family, we don't say sorry. After Martha left, one day became two. A year went by. And another. I didn't think about it much. That was the only way I could explain it. I eventually forgot about Martha. When people asked about my sister, I would say something vague. She's living in Amsterdam now.

I haven't been to Amsterdam since I was twelve years old. The year we moved to Canada. I imagined a walk with Annie around our neighbourhood. We'd have strong dark coffee at a tippy table on cobblestones. The early morning light would drop down through the bushy trees. I'd sneak a cigarette, read the newspaper, take in the city chaos; bicycles going by, musty scents of the canal, and of cannabis. See what I remembered. Then we'd visit Martha.

By 9 a.m., I grew tired of waiting for Annie to wake up. I was fidgety, awake since 5 a.m., and decided to go for a walk. The streets of the canal ring were steeper than I remembered as a boy. I thought the whole city flat and featureless then. Now I saw the streets rose and fell pleasantly. The facades of the houses along the Herengracht, the gentleman's canal, were interesting to me as an architect. I drifted along the canal admiring the houses built narrow, some tilting towards the street. Many had winches for hauling anything up that wouldn't fit through the narrow doors or up the steep staircase. Even a piano could be lifted into an attic. Nothing was impossible for the Dutch ingenuity. I crossed the bridge over the canal and saw a girl on the other side curled up on a chunk of cardboard with a torn blanket and a mutt. *Dakloos* was written on the torn box. I looked the word up on my iPhone. Homeless. I laid a handful of change at her feet. She didn't look up.

How will Martha look now? I couldn't stop thinking of cancer. The word frightened. And why not me? Fifty-three was too young. Should I buy flowers or poetry? I walked by a church where bells were sounding and then turned back, pushed the heavy wooden door open and stepped inside. I was suddenly in darkness except for a narrow light coming through slats, high in the belfry. A plaque on the wall explained the bells were a carillon, a set of twenty-three brass bells housed in the belfry. Bells that were used to notify people of wars, fires, storms and events. Someone was playing them now. The music was intimate like a voice speaking. I found myself turning my palms upward, opening them towards the belfry, as though I was offering myself in some way I'd never done before. Take me. If I die here, it's okay. Sobbing, I stayed until the piece was finished and some people entered.

Back outside, a wind swirled, stirring up dust and grit from the ground. Walking felt like I was doing something. I had the urge to keep going over the Herengracht, past Anne Frank Haus, and the Hofjes de Licht, the hospice where Martha was dying, out of the city, towards the North Sea, where the wind pushed back the land reclaimed from nothing.

Instead, I walked in the direction of the hospice, following the canal, past live-aboard boats, hip-looking coffee shops, and over a rainbow crosswalk, to the Hofjes de Licht. The hospice resembled a small temple with a pretty red gate. I half expected to see barefoot monks walking the grounds. A woman was leaving. "I like your Pelotas," she said. "Very cool."

"Thank you," I said. Was she poking fun at the way I was dressed on my way into a hospice? Too natty perhaps. She lit a cigarette and carried on. I realized I could use a cigarette and reached into my pocket. I spotted a café across the street and changed my mind about the hospice for the moment.

Later, Annie and I walked the canal ring. "Let's not get bikes until tomorrow," I said. "I'm tired and don't think I could ride a Dutch bicycle today. They have no gears. You can't stop the thing once you get going."

"No problem, Dad. I just thought it would be fun. How did it go with Auntie Martha? I was upset you went without me. I walked after you left but I didn't have an address for the hospice."

She took my hand and we walked together. I kept my failure to visit Martha to myself.

"How did you get to be so grown?" It occurred to me then Annie was the same age Martha had been when I saw her the last time.

"Time goes by. Look, a *koffiehuis*. We have to go in."

"Are you sure? I'll wait outside. You go in."

Annie bought a joint the size of a cigar and dropped it in her purse like she had purchased chewing gum.

"Tell me about Martha. I have your copy of *Ariel*."

"Sylvia Plath? You have my book?"

"Yes, Dad. Tell me the story."

"What story? There's no story."

"There is. I read what Martha wrote in your book. The death of our loved ones."

"She wrote poetry. She was dramatic. That was a long time ago."

"Cool. I write poetry too."

"You do? I had no idea."

"Do you have any of her poems?"

"No poems. I have tapes of her singing. Jazz standards, "My Funny Valentine," "How High the Moon," and some of her own compositions. You always think there will be lots of time. My fault. Anyway, let's walk back."

"Wow. I wish I'd known her. She was so talented. Dad, to-morrow we have to visit Auntie Martha."

After dinner, we sat together on the deck of our apartment and looked out at the canals below through lush treetops. I couldn't stop marvelling at how there were so many trees in the center of the city. There was one tree, larger than all the others, with small birds that flitted between branches as the sun went down.

"Tomorrow the Rijksmuseum. Sound good?" I went into the kitchen and grabbed each of us a cold Amstel from the fridge. We sat back and put our feet on the railings. Annie lit up the bazooka-sized joint, took a big puff, and handed it to me.

"Martha first, Dad. Let's visit Martha first."

I took a toke, watched the outline of her face in the near darkness. Her cropped hair. It could have been Martha. "Yes. To-morrow we'll visit Martha."

"How did you lose touch with Auntie Martha? I could have had an aunt all these years."

I swallowed a slug of beer and tried to turn thirty years of memories over.

"I know it's hard to believe. How something so small became so big. I told Martha she had to move. I think that's how I lost track of her."

"You don't sound bad," she said. "But I can kind of see Martha's side, too.

"Yeah, me too. I read once that after fourteen days if you don't fix an argument, it's no longer fixable."

"That sounds kind of harsh. I don't know. Maybe. Want another beer?"

Gusts were swirling the treetops into a frenzy. When Annie left the deck, I was despondent. Was I remembering the way it really was? The din of the street rose up. I made out voices that were just clatter before. I found myself humming. The rims of my boots tapping. There were drums sounding too, beating out a rhythm. Then the song got messy and mournful.

"Before she died, Grandma told me that Martha went home to their house after she left my place. Grandpa kicked her out.

Said she was too old to come home."

"Really? Oh no, Dad. That's bad. But I can imagine him saying that."

"Dad suspected Martha was gay. He didn't know anyone who was gay. Neither did I. Not then."

"What if I do things you don't like?"

"I don't think you could."

Wind gusted through the treetops. Annie tucked her head into my shoulder.

"I could."

At breakfast, the next day I said, "I think it's best to go to the hospice in the afternoon. It won't be busy then."

"Dad, we came all this way. Let's not wait any longer."

"Hospitals are busy in the morning. Doctors do rounds. They don't want you there. Let's rent bikes. We can cycle to the Rijksmuseum and head over to the hospice at noon."

"I think you're afraid. But anyway, noon it is." She grabbed her coat and backpack without looking at me.

"Noon. I promise."

We made it through the chaos of traffic to the Rijksmuseum. I was terrified at first, making a lot of jerky turns dodging bikes coming at me from all directions. I spent my childhood on these exact streets. How could I have forgotten?

Then we stepped into the room with the Vermeers. *The Kitchen Maid, Love Letter, Woman Reading A Letter* and *The Little Street*.

"These are nice, Dad," Annie said, as she checked the time on her phone.

I stopped in front of *Woman Reading a Letter*. The bend of her neck. Her arms raised up expecting something. I wanted to crawl into the painting, be with her. The look in her eyes, as though there had been a misunderstanding cleared up by the letter. The passing of years meant nothing. Everything eventually fell into place.

"Vermeer started his paintings with shades of grey, over which he added colour," I said. "A technique called *pointillé*. Everything was in that painting: grey morning light, sharp detail, layered colours. The woman's eagerness with the letter. Vermeer had got it right."

"What did you call it?"

Annie was on her iPhone. Checking up with friends likely.

"Sorry, I'm lecturing."

"I don't mind. You know. It's your thing. It's getting late though."

"The woman reading the letter is illuminated by light coming from her side. But do you see, there is no window in the painting."

"I don't see light on her."

"Annie, look at the wall above her and on her forehead."

Annie approached to within inches of the painting.

"I don't see it. It isn't getting any lighter." There was irritation in her voice.

"You know the poster in my office, the painting of the row houses of Delft? People say Vermeer was a master because he made the sky look like both heaven and earth in that painting. You feel the light." I was talking non-stop like I'd popped my cork and couldn't stop myself.

"Let's find that one then."

"*View of Delft* is in The Hague, not in Amsterdam."

"Too bad. I guess I don't really understand. What does that light mean?"

I backed up from the painting then and looked at Annie. Her scarf was tied around her neck twice like the young Dutch women we'd passed this morning in the street. On her sagging co-op backpack, there was a *#metoo* button.

"Are you okay, honey?"

"Yeah, why?"

"The button."

"Well, women aren't safe, Dad. That's all."

"That's all? Did I miss something?"

"No. A lady in the *koffiehuis* was giving them out. I just thought, yeah, I should wear this."

I reached into my pocket and handed Annie a button. *Take back the night.* "It's old. It was Martha's button."

"Wow. Thanks." Annie pinned the button to her pack. "That wouldn't have gone over with Grandpa."

"No."

"I still don't understand why she left."

"Maybe we'll never know for sure."

"It's late, Dad. I want to see Aunt Martha."

I rifled through my coat pocket. I couldn't find the address for the hospice. Was it on the Single or the Prinsengracht?

"We have to go back for the address, Annie."

"Jesus, Dad. You were there yesterday."

"I know. But the canals are like a maze."

We rode in silence. Took the bikes back and walked to our apartment. Annie took great strides and I tried to keep up.

"I don't even know what she has. What kind of cancer? You never said."

She was crying. I reached for her hand. She pulled away.

"What time does the hospice close? It's too late, isn't it?"

"Tomorrow. We'll go tomorrow."

"Dad, do you even know what a jerk you are?" She stomped off. I called after her. "It's my fault. I hadn't been paying attention at the museum. Time slipped away. Let's get something to eat."

After a few blocks, Annie stopped to read a flyer. "Esperanza Spalding's playing this Sunday. On the De Negen Staatjes. Where is that? Never mind. I'll find it myself."

"Who's Esperanza Spalding?"

"Jazz singer. She won a Grammy. The singer no one knew. And everyone kind of laughed when she won. Like, who's that? She's amazing."

"When we were in high school, Martha and I went to a lot of concerts together: Bowie, The Police, Dire Straits. God, we saw Aretha. We'd drive up to Pine Knob in my Cortina with the sketchy brakes, smoking dope and singing. I haven't been to a concert in years." The sky was turning rose twilight. "Let's get tickets."

"That's okay. Let's not. I don't feel like it. I want to see Martha."

"Tomorrow. Sunday morning. We'll go tomorrow."

I woke in the night sobbing and never got back to sleep. There was a weight on me like an anchor being dragged across my chest. I splashed water on my face and knocked on the door to Annie's room.

"I'm going to the hospice," I said through the door.

"Wait, I'm coming."

My heart was beating like a metronome.

Annie threw on her coat, pulled a headband over her head, grabbed her pack, and we walked into a cloudy sky, along the canal, past street people curled up in corners, past Anne Frank Haus, past the church with the carillon, all quiet this morning, through Dam Square, past the monument to the Canadians who liberated the Dutch in 1945, and over the rainbow crosswalk.

When we arrived, there was a man in the room sitting beside Martha.

"I'm from the pastoral institute," he said. "We sit with the dying, so they are never alone." Then he left abruptly. I'd been scolded. And in perfect English.

Martha was curled like a baby, her head flopped to one side. There was no IV, no high-tech machines. With pastel décor, the room was more like a place for newborns, not for the dying.

A nurse was at the door. "No fluids, and I don't think she'll wake up. She's sedated." Then she exited the room too.

I walked to the chair at the head of the bed. Annie went to the foot of the bed, slid her hands under the blanket and began rubbing Martha's feet. The way you would stroke a puppy, without asking. I sat on the edge of the chair and looked at Martha. At her closed eyes. I said my name. Once I heard myself speaking to her aloud, I became unafraid. I had the urge to lift her up and carry her out of the hospice. To the life that we should have had.

In the woolly cap, Martha looked young. The way I remembered her. I unbuttoned my coat and lifted her hand. She felt dry and papery and warm. I ran my fingertips across the top of her hand, along the knuckles and bony arches of fingers. In our family, we did not touch. I moved over her wrist and up her forearm. I clutched her, like a starving thrush, and then dropped her arm, terrified that I would hurt her.

I lifted her hand again. I looked at her face and saw there Martha from when we were children. She opened her mouth and licked her lips.

"What should we do, Annie? The nurse said no fluids."

"It can't hurt, Dad. She's dying.

"What if we're wrong?"

"She's thirsty. Give her some water."

There were little sponges on sticks on the table. I plunged one of them into a cup of water and laid it at her lips. She took it like a hungry fledgling. I fed her another and another.

"She's cold, Dad." Annie took off her coat and stretched it across Martha's legs and feet.

Then Martha's lunch arrived. "Why would they bring her food if she can't eat? She doesn't even know we're here." I wanted a medical opinion about what to do. There was no one to ask. So, I asked Martha.

"There is a dessert. Would you like some raspberry custard?" I looked back at Annie. She was vigorously rubbing Martha's feet.

"Martha loved raspberries. Just a tiny bite, Martha. It's good," I said, and slid the baby-sized spoon into her mouth. Martha sat up, opened her mouth, and licked the custard off the tiny spoon. She ate effortlessly. I expected her to open her eyes, but she didn't. Then she dropped her head back down onto the pillow. I put my face to her face the way I used to put my nose right up to Annie's nose when she was an infant sleeping. To make sure she was breathing. There was the littlest bit of air, like a soft mist, slow and laboured, in and out. Annie came and pushed me over so that we were both sitting squished together on the chair.

Light slid into the room, up the length of Martha, over Annie and me. This was no ordinary light. It was light breaking through a cloudy sky, through trees, from the heavens, light from the past. Annie went back to the foot of the bed and laid her hands on Martha's feet. Then she began to sing. "Comes a Time." I started singing too. The light kept coming, overpowering the low light of the hospice. Then it was gone as fast as it came. When I turned around, Annie was gone too. There were Martha and me. I put my nose to Martha's nose.

We left the hospice and walked. Lights were coming on seeping through windows of the canal houses. There was a chill in the autumn air. I took Annie's hand. She squeezed mine.

"The years just passed straight by me, Annie."

"Where should we go, Dad? Maybe there's a church?"

"There is a church. Back on the Herengracht. I was there two days ago."

"You were?"

This seemed to surprise Annie. "With bells like someone singing from the belfry. The music. Would that be good?"

"Yeah, totally. Maybe I could read a poem."

"That would be perfect."

We hugged our coats around us, both of our chins wet from tears. A gust of rain arrived, rustled the trees. We walked, across canals, up and down rolling streets, over the rainbow crosswalk, dodged bicycles and people strolling arm in arm, and past De Negen Staatjes and a funky version of "Autumn Leaves" drifting through the night air. Falling into a rhythm. Into the pearly grey Amsterdam light.

Between the Heron and the Wren

Day becomes night. Stars will come. Moon will rise. In the world we shared, I wrote these opening words for an opera my brother composed. In this way, we used our art to look after each other.

It is late autumn, after work, and I'm riding my bike to yoga. Rain comes in an unrelenting drizzle on the West Coast this time of year. Only the hardy are cycling still. There is just enough light as we cyclists pass each other in our bright coloured rain jackets, water dripping off our hands and noses. Riding my bike feels fine this late in the season, a miraculous feeling of wind skimming my skin and the sweet pungent scent of the earth sodden with rain. I ride past the jumbled last surviving plantings of the children's garden with the small sign stating who tended it today. Though it looks past tending. A dog barking, someone sings, the chords of the season. It's comforting to see people going by on their own journeys. I want to go slow. I want to live in the moment. There are only so many moments left. I know this now.

Everybody loved my brother, his blue eyes, his clear voice when he spoke, his grace. Above all, he was loved for his intellect, his strong will and his vocation. And for his wit. Who else would roll dice to score an opera? My brother was also sensitive and even small insults would open wounds and soak him in sweat and worry. So, he wandered his own path with his turmoil and his thirst for knowledge.

It would have been easy for such a life to come to ruin. But over the decades his life changed. The small boy who never sat for a photo without a furrowed brow left his home and revealed himself to be a peaceful warrior. As he studied and wrote and his works were performed, other musicians understood his genius and revered him. He found love too. And the landscape of his life changed. Until day became night.

Though I take the bikeway, I must pay attention. On a steep hill where I pick up speed, there are fissures in the pavement, and I half wonder if the forks of my old bike won't crumple. There are places where the city traffic passes and even on these small side streets the clamor startles me. Every time I pass the school, children are crossing, busy with chatter, not looking up, ignoring the crossing guard.

As soon as I settle into a rhythm, the cadence of the wheels spinning, my mind is off on its own wandering, naming the things I pass. Small wooden bridge. Lamppost I never saw before. Graffiti: The end of the world is nigh. Squirrels in a hurry. Red maple trees blazing in a last dance. Lovers meandering. When I name familiar things, it tames my fear. The way children don't step on a crack in the sidewalk. Asking God for something. Keep my loved ones safe.

It's up to me. My younger brother is dying. We're all dying. I know this. But he's not old enough to die.

On any day now, I'll be cycling and all at once the light around me grows dim. The first time this happened, I thought my eyes were failing. Suddenly everywhere there was darkness. Dark clouds gathering. Light fading on the horizon. An unsettling quiet in the valley. Above me, the canopy of trees casts long shadows. The draft of cool air: Was this now an underworld? The very fact of death. I read that grief and sorrow can take you to a place where the earth opens and the world beneath reveals its secrets.

After I've crossed over the busy roads, I get to the place where I cycle with the creek to my right. It's wild and gusting. The water foams ferocious and roars—winter is coming. Leaves seem dumbstruck, as they are ripped from branches, spinning in a flurry to the ground.

I see a heron standing alone on the marshy shoreline. There isn't really time to stop, but I do. Then I notice there are two herons, one in the air, squawking and nudging the other bird. Immediately, I get off my bike to look closer and for lack of a better explanation, I think they're having a tiff with each other. I don't dare encroach on their territory, but then I do, stepping slowly, nearer and nearer, until I see one is actually pecking at the other. Watching is irresistible. I'm not certain of anything, but I think the elder is telling the fledgling it's time to find its own way. Forcing the leaving that the young bird resists. It isn't calling, just stretching its neck gazing at the elder bird.

My brother was defenseless as a kid. He needed a guide. The simple explanation is that he was sickly as a child, sensitive and smart. The way he would wade in deep water but expect a parent would make him safe. Our parents were always busy, so I was in charge of him. He trusted me and I looked after him. I read books to him at bedtime. He'd sit with his head on my lap, listening, looking at the pictures. But he would be afraid to fall asleep. Afraid of darkness, beasts and unhappy endings. All those nights I would make up different endings to the stories. I even gave "The Little Match Girl" a home to go to and parents who loved her. "Aren't you changing the ending?" he'd ask. As though he knew fairy tales usually had disturbing endings. "No, that's exactly right," I'd say. We read that story a hundred times and I never let her die. Not once.

It's late. I get back on my bike and push my legs like pistons, working up a sweat. I have crossed my own landscape too. My own unsettling encounter with near death. There aren't many people that come to you in your darkness and offer light. But in that time, my brother asked me to be his librettist.

"Does that have one 't' or two?" I'd said. There was something in what he'd asked that was so big. He'd seen things in me I could not see in myself.

"What opera?" I asked.

"I want to do *Siddhartha*. The story by Herman Hesse."

"Oh, I read that. Ages ago. Classic story of a young man leaving home and going into the world. I could relate to that."

"What did you like?" he asked.

"Well, that it was so difficult for him to leave his father and his best friend behind. I read it when I was nineteen. I understood his longing."

"How old were you when you left home?" he asked.

"Nineteen."

"The same age as Siddhartha."

"Yeah."

"I was twelve when you left. You were there one day and gone the next. After that, I had no one."

"We're supposed to go. That's what kids do. Grow up and leave."

Then he leaned in close and whispered into my ear, "Siddhartha met his river too. He crossed it twice. Once as a young man. Then again, late in his life."

"Oh," I said. "I don't think I knew that."

"You can do it," he said.

"Libretto," I say now, letting the *o* linger and roll off of my tongue until it sounds soft and round and flowed as the river. I rub my hands along the smooth surface of the handlebars, taking the helm with a marvellous precision, my eyes fixed on what lay ahead. Riding the current as I pick up speed.

By the time I reach the hill to the yoga studio, it's late. I lock my bike. The door is already closed so I will have to wait now for the next class or give up and go home. It will be pitch dark on the ride home if I stay. The staff at the front desk thinks I can't read the schedule. "You're late," she says, shaking her head. "I guess mistakes happen."

"I know," I say, coolly. "Mistakes happen."

In fact, it's the opposite, I've been coming to this class for years and I've never been late before. Outside, I can hear the rain growing heavy. I was never a patient person, but I know how much I need this hour, so I take a seat and wait.

When the door finally opens for the following class, I roll out my yoga mat and select my props from the shelf. People are talking but I don't look at anyone. Soon we are sitting on our mats as the instructor introduces himself. "My name is Miguel, I'll be your guide," he says, with calmness, like a voice from an old-time movie. He's not my regular teacher. He lights incense and places a small gong at his side. New-agey. Tonight, I really don't care. We sit in lotus position and the music begins. I follow, raise my hands to my heart. It's so easy. Chant *Om* together before we begin. Chanting through my own awkwardness. Surrender.

Slowly, we begin to move. With breath, we pick up speed, legs and arms accelerate in and out of the asana poses, adjusting weight, knees bend and straighten. Effortlessly lifting and dropping down, I am retracing my steps. Following the stream of my own knowledge. I'm floating without words; crossing to the other side of the river.

Some people come onto this planet with goodness. And perhaps not for a long time. My brother moved to the States to study and he's been teaching music at a university there. He travelled such a long way to find his place in the world where he made a life in song. Later, when he was older, he called on me. In time, we created that opera and a ballet and stories and poems together. Things he asked of me. Things I could never imagine we could do.

Then one day he got lost driving home from the university where he teaches. He downplayed the mishap. But that's the day the moon broke open. How suddenly it happens. The earth forms and takes.

As we near the end of class, the group returns to lotus position. The room has fallen dark and silent. I see light arcing through the room. Like in a dream. It stays with me for a while. Siddhartha, once as immovable as a tree, rises to sing. He circles the room like a dancer singing to himself and to the river. *Day becomes night. Stars will come. Moon will rise.* Time stretches and shrinks. I am singing *Om.* Not one, but many *Oms.* I sing as though I am the only one in the room singing. Singing from an unlocked place within. Chanting *accelerando.*

Again, light sweeps through the room, this time settling onto my lap. He is here, the child, beaming radiant, his head resting on a pillow, his books heaped on the floor. I stroke his hair. He doesn't speak, but he holds my hand. I have feared this moment. This scrolling back. My heart expands; seamlessly light enters and the child vanishes. All of a sudden, the room is hot. I trace the ridges of my own hand, stopping at every turn, the places he stopped for me. Places lost and found again. The bridge of peace. Talking to the moonlight. Strings and woodwinds, elegant and witty. I am at the river helping my brother's boat across. But the story isn't mine. It is the man's score that floats on the water, the one who slips alone into the river of shimmering stillness. "Safe journey home," I say, in a hushed voice.

The trail is empty. I ride my bike more slowly through the dark hour, though my bicycle has a map of its own tonight. Leaves are still falling. The creek is still rushing through the valley. I pass the place where the herons were and wonder if they've settled their spat. Then I gather my speed trying to stay warm.

When I come to the woods, I veer off the paved bikeway and take the path into the park with the towering Douglas firs, Sitka spruce and hemlocks. There is a section of old-growth where I would take my brother when he visited. I watched then as his shoulders dropped and his furrowed brow smoothed, struck by the way the woods seemed to brighten and recharge his spirit. It should be dark, but it is not. Every minute the light turns to me. I hear the loud chattering of a winter wren and stop to look. The little rotund songbird scampers along a dead fir tree, churring with vigor. I say his name. Suddenly I am shuddering tears onto the already damp mulch of the forest's understory. Treetops creak and the little wren looks up at me, unfazed. The lulling reprise of the rain. The wind like small bells diminishing beasts. The very thought of you.

SIMPLE GIFTS

Something was wrong with the tempo. The windshield wipers had been set to *allegro*, but they delayed, stopped all together and started clapping *presto*. The swiftness agitated Alexandra. She was *adagio;* compressed and sustained. Her eyes stinging, dried out from sobbing.

She felt for the controls. Turn signal, cruise, rear wiper. Jesus. Driving her dad's car seemed like a good idea this morning when she left Vancouver for Coquitlam, a suburb thirty kilometres outside the city. Now she wished someone else was in control. Dad. She glanced around. Cars and trucks were bearing down on her at excessive speed. Tailgating, merging, changing lanes. If Dad were here, they would be laughing at the craziness of modern life. He'd be telling stories, describing his favourite imaginary propeller until soon they would seem to be flying over top of the traffic. But Dad wasn't here. Dad was gone. Burned in a fire only five days ago with Mom. Now she was an orphan. She repeated these words aloud. She couldn't explain anything. The sky was dark. It was eight o'clock in the morning on Friday, December 30. What had her dad been thinking? Why not choose a lawyer in Vancouver?

The radio was tuned to CBC when Alexandra started the car and she made no effort to change it. Her dad only listened to classical music. *It's more intelligent, Alex.* Everything outside the car was swishing clutter. Inside, a solo cello began to play. Her ragged breathing slowed to *grave.* She recognized the piece. Memories came and she wanted to close her eyes and let them flood over her. Her life was the cello. Her language was music. She had to pull the car over off the freeway. Somehow.

As she listened, her body lifted out of the darkness. Warmth like a hot stone filled her insides and at that moment she felt her mom and dad were with her. She unzipped her down jacket. When the music stopped, the announcer and a guest began a repartee.

"That was Edward Elgar's 'Cello Concerto in E minor,' made famous by Jacqueline du Pré."

"Yes, and did you know du Pré was only twenty years old when she played with Elgar conducting?" asked the guest.

"No," said the announcer.

The guest continued, *deciso*. "The wonderfully talented du Pré, would go on to develop MS at age twenty-eight, and be dead at the age of forty-two. A real tragedy."

There was silence. The announcer said almost nothing. As though he didn't know what to say. Sad mess that. Poor Jacqueline du Pré. What could anyone say?

The rain was not letting up. The passenger side mirror was folded in like an envelope. She reached over to push it out, started the car, and eased herself back onto the freeway. Alexandra was twenty years old. Soon she was hurtling along, her attention lapsed, and she drifted into the next lane. A pickup truck laid on his horn. She should have stayed in Toronto. Not taken the call. *Your parents are dead.*

She had been lying awake in bed, idly staring out the window, when the call came. A storm had blown all night. She watched the last leaves on the maple trees outside her window rustle and fly through the sky like swallows murmuring. Black spaces moved briskly through the clouds and a rosy light formed off in the distance when her cell phone rang. She noted the time: 7:09 a.m. She didn't recognize the number but picked it up anyway, because she was curious.

"Hello, Alexandra. Are you awake? It's Marty and Hal." The Johnsons, her parents' best friends. Both of them were on the phone together, on a speaker, too loud in her quiet suite.

"There's been a fire. We're so sorry."

"What?" she asked, in the way one does not need to ask more. She clenched her iPhone and lifted herself up off the pillow and straightened her back.

"Your parents are both gone."

"Gone?" Her voice murmured.

There was a long flat silence. "Dead. Died. They died." Hal Johnson stumbled over his words. Coughed. His voice was breaking. Up. Down. She could barely hear him. He cleared his throat. "There was a fire. Last night. They are both dead."

"Come home, sweetie." That was Marty trying to sound normal. "Come home and be with us."

"Does Charlie know?" Alexandra asked. She braced herself. There was a calmness in her that grew large in times of chaos. Would the Johnsons even know how to reach her brother?

"Not yet. No."

"I'll call him," she said. She couldn't bear the thought of her brother receiving this same phone call. "Thanks for calling."

Someone was honking a car horn incessantly in the street below her studio. She had a sudden urge to get off the phone. She couldn't think. Her small room seemed even smaller. She wanted to slouch back onto her pillow. Go back to sleep. Turn back time. But she didn't. She was becoming agitated.

She climbed out of bed, pulled on her robe, and washed her face. She did not want to phone her brother in Cologne, Germany. She made coffee. Her brother was like a stranger to her. An hour passed. The room swayed. Her small high-ceilinged room was small, almost empty. She'd taken nothing from home when she left Vancouver. She sat at the table and lined up the edges of her few books; One Hundred Years of Solitude, Death of a Naturalist and Woolgathering. All more appealing than what she had to do. Then she made the call.

Charlie was at work. She would get to the point. There's been a fire. As soon as he said hello, the second she heard his voice, she started to weep uncontrollably. Hunched and sobbing she saw herself standing up to her neck in ashes. Their ashes. The ashes of their house. Her family.

"Charlie, Mom and Dad are dead. They died last night. Our house burned down." She blurted all this out and went quiet. Sunlight poured through the window, but she was cold. It was winter and there were tiny flakes of snow blowing past the window.

There was a long silence. "Are you there? Talk to me," she said.

"I'm here." More silence.

"The Johnsons just phoned. That's all I know. Can you fly home through Toronto? We could fly back to Vancouver together. Please."

She folded her fingers nervously around the belt of her bathrobe and waited for his reply. Her brother had fallen out of her life when he moved to Cologne to work at Max Planck. She was thirteen at the time and too young to know him.

"Yes, of course. I'll book a flight in the morning." He was formal with her. So distant.

"Charlie, I need you."

"Right. Well, I can't do anything now until morning. I'll let you know."

Charlie flew through Toronto and they made the trip on to Vancouver together.

"You know that house was a firetrap. Old electrical wiring and Dad always doing his own repairs, jerry-rigging everything."

They went to the house together. It seemed like a good idea. As soon as she came to the police tape, she felt woozy. The smell of smoke and blackened rubble overwhelming.

"I'm going over to the Johnsons, don't stay here too long. Please."

She left Charlie walking through the burned house. With the Johnsons she made a list: call the funeral home, the minister, order flowers, coffee and sandwiches. The Johnsons sent out an e-mail to her parents' friends. She chose the music for the service.

At the church, Alex mingled and talked to everyone. When Mrs. Johnson walked out of the church kitchen, she was wearing her mom's apron, the one with appliquéd maple leaves. Alexandra trembled. She didn't have anything that her mother had made. Her mom was crafty. Never called what she did art. When the service was over, she asked for the apron. That night, utterly exhausted, she fell asleep with the apron rolled up in a ball on her belly.

She drove her brother to the airport the next day. The Johnsons had offered to drive her to the lawyer's office, but when she saw Dad's wagon, she had the idea to drive his car to the appointment. His car was all that was left. She wanted to be inside the vehicle by herself. Smell his pipe tobacco, unroll one of his mints, finger his pencils, read his notes stuck to the dash. Roll her eyes at the maps piled up on the passenger seat and floor. Driving with her dad used to make her happy when she wasn't.

"Life can be a challenge. Nearly impossible. Then you look at those trees. Eh, kiddo?" He couldn't help pointing out every little thing. He saw detail in the world that other people missed. And always wonder.

The problem was that she rarely ever drove anymore. Her life was buses, subways, or walking. She'd only driven the wagon once. Her head was pounding faster than the metronomic swoosh of the wipers. Every vehicle in Vancouver seemed to be enroute to Coquitlam this morning, a suburb she had never even been to before. She stole a quick glance at herself in the rearview mirror. Her long hair dyed platinum. The small ring through her nose and one through her eyebrow. Suddenly her looks felt eccentric. She'd been good with her appearance at the service. But she wasn't feeling right this morning for the lawyer.

Only a week ago, Alexandra had been a master's student on a music scholarship at the University of Toronto. She felt she was finally on the fast track. Her mentor, Dr. Lorna MacDonald had said, "Alexandra, one day you will play the cello like Yo-Yo Ma." Alexandra was embarrassed by the compliment. It was a wild exaggeration, but she held onto those words all the same, stowing them like a talisman. Yo-Yo Ma had played at Obama's inauguration. He played with Sting. He played in Steve Jobs' living room, and at his memorial. Yo-Yo Ma had made the cello cool again.

She had done everything, hadn't she? With the help of the Johnsons, and very little help from Charlie she had made all the arrangements. Done a good job, too. The people at the service all said so. She didn't cry until she played "Sarabande." Then it flowed out of her, untethering. Emptied and set adrift in the music. Now she was driving to meet her dad's lawyer to find out what she should do next. They would go over the will. She had no idea what that meant. She was exhausted and strung out on caffeine.

Watching the exit signs, Alexandra tried to focus. She was already in the slower right lane and exited the freeway with no problem. The lawyer's office was in a shopping mall across the overpass. There was nothing else there except a long beige building with an enormous empty parking lot.

The minute she sat down across from the lawyer she began vibrating. He was a middle-aged man and he had a slim file folder open on the desk in front of him. He talked about probate, and appraising the land, and assets and taxes. She did not understand a word he was saying. She clutched her hands on her lap to still her shaking. The rose tattoo on the back of her hand began to swirl. She pulled her skirt to cover a hole in her tights. What am I doing here? She might fly right out the window of the half-furnished office.

He looked up at her and closed the file folder. "I'll tell you what," he said. "We'll finish everything by the end of the week and get you back to school again. How does that sound?"

"It's Friday. It's already the end of the week." She was irritated and tired and immediately sorry that she had snapped at him.

"Where's your brother?"

"He's gone back to Cologne." She shifted her feet trying to calm herself. She could not seem to get enough air into her lungs.

"Well, the estate will be divided between you and your brother. There's nothing more you can do now.

"Do you have funds for school?" he asked. He talked at her right shoulder, not to her face.

"No," she said.

"Well, there was some money in the bank. Not much, I'm afraid. I'll set up an account for you."

When he showed her to the door, he stood too long, like he was looking for words he could not find. He shook her hand. "Unthinkable," he said. Then he turned and walked back into his office.

The entire appointment had lasted only fifteen minutes. As she departed the law office for the street in front where she had parked her dad's Audi, Alexandra turned around and began walking in reverse. At a moderate pace she walked backwards through the doorway and then faster. *What a jerk.* The money thing had her worried. She was starting to feel slightly dreamy and loopy. A hand that did not seem like her hand opened the car door. Her body sat down in the driver's seat. She grabbed the banana bread, shovelled it into her mouth and washed it down with the cold latte. Her iPhone was dead. She wanted to crank up Arcade Fire's *Funeral.* All the way back to Vancouver, rain rolled across the windshield.

As soon as she departed the suburb, Alexandra began losing her life in Vancouver with Mom and Dad and Charlie. All the birthdays, Halloweens, Christmases. The stucco house on Courtney Street. Twenty years of film bleached into blankness, with no final words. No good-bye. That life, wherever it was now, had quit her. She scrolled backwards until there was nothing left. Did she have health insurance, she wondered? There were a lot of bad drivers out here.

When she pulled up to the Johnsons' house, they were at the front door, waiting for her. Mrs. Johnson was waving. "How'd it go, honey?"

She couldn't think of a single thing to say. She was afraid she might say something nasty. She might scream. One more night and she would be on a flight home to Toronto. She made a gesture of thanks and walked in the door.

On the flight back to Toronto she dozed, listened to music, tried to watch a movie. At some point, in the fog of the night, she was sitting on a wooden pew in the St. Agnes Church in Kotham, Germany. She had never been to Germany. She was wearing a long blue dress appliquéd with maple leaves. Light was forcing its way through a window of yellow stained glass into the chapel. Yo-Yo Ma was seated in front of the pulpit. She was close enough to touch him. He was playing Bach's "Cello Suites" and staring at her. The music made her calm. There was a creaking sound above his head. When she looked up, she saw great curved wooden beams supporting the peaked roof, each one bent into the shape of a heart. In her lap, her fingers were in nimble motion, *dolce,* across an imaginary fingerboard.

She was sixteen years old when she began to play the cello. She had fretted about this. Sixteen was too old. Yo-Yo Ma started when he was four. Once she had decided, she became focused right away, finding a teacher, setting her alarm clock to practise at 5 a.m. That year, while her friends were listening to Arctic Monkeys, Alexandra was in her bedroom scratching "Twinkle Twinkle Little Star" across the coarse strings and wanting nothing more than to pull the bow flawlessly. Striving for grace. *Grazioso.* All she thought about when she finished the piece was starting over again.

The next morning, back in her rented room on the third floor of the blue house on Brunswick Avenue in the University Annex, Alexandra opened her eyes to a new year. She shivered under her quilt but could not seem to muster the energy to drag herself out of bed to turn up the heat. Instead she rummaged the room with her eyes. She was becoming invisible. Her books were stacked neatly on the trestle table. Her clothes were hanging, arranged by colour, on a wire clothesline that her boyfriend Jeremy had made for her, her cello leaned in its place against the warmest inside wall. Everything was as she had left it. She should be consoled by this. She was not.

From her bed she could see the first hint of the sky becoming light. The trees in Jean Sibelius Square were skeletons, thin and reaching. The pointed top of University College looked like a sharp object poking through skin. During the night, long and fierce with tossing and turning, and wide awake, she had felt herself plummeting into the muted deep.

In three days, classes would start back. She should e-mail her professors, but her thoughts were too scrambled. She was holding tight to an image of a girl, hair in a tight ponytail, twelve or thirteen, writing resolutions in a pink spiral notebook. Making New Year's resolutions was what her family did. Fix this, fix that.

Her eyes were drawn to the ceiling. She had not really noticed the painted wooden beams of her studio before, angled to the roof. Simple, not the elegant curved beams in the St. Agnes church, but there was something there. How had she missed this before? She was lying in bed, wrapped in a blue quilt appliquéd with maple leaves. She could smell fir branches and fruit and candle wax. Tears formed. Her parents no longer existed. The memory of the pink spiral notebook slid away into the light of morning.

She coaxed herself out of her creaking bed. Her bleached hair was hanging in knots and a pain knifed across her temples. From habit, she flexed her fingers and stretched her arms over her head, attending to the lean small muscles of her body she needed for playing. Setting her pitch. She was hungry and knew without looking that the fridge was empty. She made herself a cup of strong coffee, her hands shook and fumbled. Across the room, a thin ray of light angled off the surface of the window glass and into her eyes and for a second she was blinded. In the moment of darkness something cracked. She hurled the cup across the room. She had the urge to trash everything, not make any resolutions. Not one.

She chose a heavy wool sweater that belonged to Jeremy and pulled it over her head, zipped her down coat. She texted Jeremy. She was jittery with hunger and panicky about being alone. Jeremy would calm her down. He was the one person who would. She could eat at the Brunswick House if she walked over to the campus. She moved past her cello and made her way down the wooden stairs of her apartment. The old steps tilted so that she had to walk on her tiptoes to keep from falling. Without noticing, she turned around and exited the front door backwards.

She banged into the garden gate and almost fell into the hedge, coming face to face with a Japanese maple that was not yet bare. Why wasn't it bare? Even the leaves that had fallen to the ground did not look dead. She bent to pick up a single red maple leaf, shimmering with freshness. She pushed it into her pocket. She set off slowly, leaning into the wind. It was starting to snow. She had not eaten since the flight yesterday. Jeremy answered her text. He'd meet her at The Brunswick. But within minutes she heard his unmistakable whistling coming towards her. The familiar sound of him was uplifting. She ran and threw her body into him.

"I'm glad you're back," he said. "It's cold, eh?"

Everything bottled up for the past week leaked out. She was crying again. Jeremy yanked the brim of his tweed cap low on his forehead and buried his nose in her face; both of them sobbed.

"Okay," she said and wriggled out of the hug. "I want to feel good this morning. Let's walk. You were whistling. Whistle for me."

"Are you joking? It's minus-twelve degrees. Let's just get over to campus and get inside. Can I ask you one thing? I don't know what you played at the service."

"Sting's 'Fragile,' Bach's 'Cello Suite Number Six' and at the end, 'Sarabande.'"

"Wow. 'Fragile.' Nice. Sting for your mom and Bach for your dad. Right? And Sara what?"

"'Sarabande.' It's Bach too. I played that for me. As my good-bye. It's an unbearably sad farewell. I think it's the saddest but most spiritual piece Bach wrote. If you can have both of those in one piece. Like searching for a light to return home by."

"Cool," he said.

They walked in silence the rest of the way to The Brunswick. Once inside they ordered breakfast. She ate eggs and turkey sausages and toast and a slice of orange, cleaning her plate. She did not mention her Christmas again. It was as though they'd both agreed to have something not so dark. Jeremy told funny stories about his Christmas holiday in Florida. After breakfast they pulled on their winter coats, Jeremy took her hand and they walked back to her apartment.

"I've got a seminar this evening," he said.

"You do? It's New Year's Day."

"I know. Some of us volunteered for a psychology study. And it's the only night everyone could make it. Sorry. You'll be okay? You could come."

She rolled her eyes. "Of course not. But I'll manage. I might take a few days off. Start classes next week. What d'ya think?"

"School goes back on Wednesday."

"I know."

At the door he kissed her. *Tenerezza.* He hovered on the porch, leaning into her like a cat. She should ask him in, but they would smoke a joint and it would progress to sex, and she was afraid of her reaction. She couldn't imagine taking her clothes off either. She was frozen. Already she was shrinking.

"Maybe you should practise," he said.

"I'm kind of tired. I might take a nap."

"What about that kid who wants lessons?"

"Caterina Russo?" She let go of his hand.

"You could call her?"

"I don't know." Her eye began twitching. "That's a big commitment."

"What? You promised her."

"She could find someone else." She looked over his shoulder into the park. The afternoon light was touching the horizon. She reached into her pocket for the maple leaf.

She was drowsy and fell asleep and did not wake until it was dark, her iPhone ringing. It was the mother of Caterina Russo. She was speaking too fast. *Con brio.* Alexandra had no intention of saying yes to her. But then she could hear herself saying yes.

In her room it was quiet and cold. She wished she had a fireplace. She rewound herself in the blue quilt, fell asleep again, and dreamed of Christmas pudding, dark, steaming, tipped and turned upside down on a platter, with brandy pouring down the top, over the edges. Her mother made the best Christmas pudding. How was her mother?

She pushed herself out of bed, hesitated, then walked across the room to her cello and unzipped the case. Handling the top of her cello, she took in the aroma of the lacquered spruce. Her hand scrolled along the curve of the upper bout, up the stretched and slender neck, to the pegs and around the top. The cello is tall with the hourglass shape of a beautiful woman. A humming dark timbre sighed, arriving from deep in the well of the insides. She laid the instrument on the floor and rested her ear on the f-hole. A woman's voice trembling through the belly of the cello. Streetlights shone through the window, across the room.

"You are lovely," she said, stroking the curved edges like long silken hair. Once she began, she did not know how to stop. Into the shadows, she ran her cheek, outlining the silhouette: the neck, the shoulder, the belly. Flushed and hurrying. Something in her was colliding. She stretched her arms across the breadth of the instrument, until they were lying, skin to skin. "Come home." Finally, exhausted, she dropped her hands, buried her face in the curving bout, closed her eyes and fell asleep.

In the morning the pain was back, sharper than yesterday. Sharper than the day before yesterday. The unbearable aching fog of loneliness.

It was stuffy in her room, almost impossible to breathe. She must take a shower and meet Caterina Russo. She opened the window. A bird burst in through the opening. A blazing shot of red cardinal glided from the bed to the table, alighting on the clothesline. Curious, Alexandra did nothing. The cardinal started to panic, ramming itself into the wall, trying to escape the room. Alexandra put down her toothbrush and opened her arms, like wings, trying to herd the bird towards the window, but the frightened bird took to the ceiling and would not come down.

"Just breathe, little one," she said. *Moderato.* She looked for something to dislodge the bird, found the broom and with the bristled end gently lifted the bird in the direction of the open window. The cardinal flew out the opening, back into the sky.

Alexandra rang the doorbell of the prettiest house on the street. A house like a storybook house. There were pebbles and planters and on the front door a fir bough so big a dad would have to have hung it there. As soon as she rang the bell, she felt like an orphan girl from a Grimm's fairy tale at the front door of the kind of house people call lovely. Then the door swung open and there was a girl half her size.

"I've been waiting for you," said the girl.

"I'm Alexandra. Do you just open the door to anybody?"

"I knew it would be you. You have cool hair."

The teacher stood on the porch examining her pupil. She noted Caterina Russo was small. Perhaps she was growing, but she was too small for a full-height cello.

"Pleased to meet you Alex-sand-ra." The child reached out her tiny hand. "Follow me to the music room. Are you coming every day?"

"No. Not every day." She unzipped her coat, rewound and knotted her scarf and followed the girl down the hallway. "How tall are you, Caterina?"

"I'm four-foot-one, I'm eight years old and I'm in grade three at General Wolfe Elementary School. And in case you want to know, I'm a Capricorn and my favourite book is *Harry Potter and The Philosopher's Stone.*"

She had not imaged her new student. This little girl with perfect diction, perfect posture and a long wavy ponytail of red hair the colour of cayenne peppers. As they sat together in the middle of the music room with its windows on three sides, Alexandra thought she was going to implode. She could not remember anything so beautiful. The room smelled of spring. Like something blooming. Crocus or snowdrops. I can do this, she said to herself. *Poco a poco.*

"I'm just thinking about your cello."

"You think it's too big for me. Don't you?" Caterina lifted the cello, settling it into her small hands. Small hands that seemed to grow longer and strong and confident as she positioned her cello. Then she raised her head, relaxed into the instrument and glanced up at Alexandra. "I'm ready."

Alexandra's mouth fell open as she watched the child. "Well, it's not too big for you," she laughed.

"Dad says there are three rules."

"Oh, only three?"

"Yes Alex-sand-ra. Three rules you have to remember. Do you want to know what they are?" She was smiling and bouncy and looked like she was about to jump to her feet.

"Of course, but stay where you are."

Caterina wrapped her arms around the neck of her cello, the way a child hugs a doll, and began. "Number one is work hard. Number two is dream a dream." Her eyes were exclamation marks. "And number three is have fun."

"Do you have a dream, Caterina?"

"Oh yes. I'm going to play the cello for the prime minister. And for JK Rowling. That's who wrote *Harry Potter.* And for you. I have to learn everything. Every kind of music."

"How did you choose the cello?"

"I was watching on television when it was President Obama's first big day, outside, in the cold. There was a man playing a song for all the people. I thought he was playing a really big violin. He looked like the happiest man in the whole wide world."

"Do you know who that man was?"

"Yes. Yo-Yo Ma. He went to Juilliard."

"What do you want to play?"

"My favourite song is 'Born This Way.' I like 'Eleanor Rigby' and 'Free Fallin'.' The one John Mayer sings. I like Elton John and Madonna. I'm learning Bach's 'Prelude for Unaccompanied Cello,' but I can't do the thumb yet."

Caterina talked so fast the room crackled with electricity. A ball of light glowed around her. Alexandra paused. Her eyes were stinging, and her heart began beating too fast. *Agitado.* Every instinct in her said to turn and run. She had promised Caterina's mother and sitting in front of her was a child expecting her lesson. Finally, she rubbed her forehead.

"Let's start with the 'Prelude' then."

Caterina began to play. She made some mistakes with her fingering, but she was surprisingly good with the bow, sparingly, like a feather.

"What's your favourite colour, Caterina?"

"Red. I love love love everything red," she said, pushing back her ponytail.

"All right then. Let's put some red dots on your cello. The dots will help you remember where to put your fingers."

"Great," she said. "I have to give it my best shot. Don't I?"

"Yes, you do," Alexandra said.

By the end of the lesson, Alexandra did not want to leave the sunny, charged music room with the small leaded windows, creamy walls, shelves of books and the aroma of vegetable soup coming from the kitchen. During the hour of the lesson it was as though she had been covered over with an ointment. *Lamentoso.* She picked up her books and folder and quietly said good-bye.

On Saturday night Jeremy showed up at her door with pizza, beer and his chessboard. He didn't talk much. She couldn't concentrate on chess, so they watched a movie. It was nice. He didn't seem to want anything.

"How's it going with that kid?" he asked.

"I can't teach anyone," she said. "She's eight. That's young."

"Well, don't discriminate against her because of her age," he said. "What does she know?"

"Teaching is too hard."

"But not impossible," he said. "And by the way, when are you coming back to class?"

"I don't know," she said.

"It's been two weeks, Alex. You'll never catch up. Come to the study. The subjects are like you."

"All depressed?"

"Well, yes. But of course. You've been through a trauma."

She watched his mouth moving. He was lecturing her. It sounded like he was singing. Her room was too cold. She wrapped her scarf tighter around her neck. The muscles in her head were rumbling. She began breathing so quickly she was going to splinter apart. He was murmuring in her ear. "Babe, you need help." Wind carried his voice away. She pulled the blue quilt over her head. Curling into herself. His voice was only a song.

When she woke up, she was alone. She did not open the case of her cello. She did not go to class. But she will make it to her lesson. She fumbled with her things: music, notes, pencil, folder. She surprised herself. She was looking forward to the lesson.

They had a pattern already. The lessons began with the Bach 'Prelude.' As Caterina took her seat and began to play, Alexandra looked out the window, tapped her foot, and listened. Caterina began slowly. But in no time, she was playing fast. Too fast. *Vivace.* Like everything in the room was going to rattle and break. Like she was going to explode.

"Do you know Jónsi?" Alexandra asked.

"Yes, Alex-sand-ra. I love Jónsi."

"Well, sometimes he uses a cello bow to play guitar. He said when he's bowing, he closes his eyes, and imagines he is riding a really wild horse and he has to tame the horse. Not frighten it."

"I'm playing too fast?" she asked.

"Yes. A little. You could ease up on the reins."

Caterina clapped her hands with delight. "Can I do it again? I'm going to tame my horse.

"How is this?" she asked, her cadences eased into the melody.

The next morning, Alexandra was in the bathroom when she heard the door of her apartment open. It was Jeremy, whistling and carrying a canvas grocery bag.

"Groceries?"

"Yeah, Babe. Well, you don't have anything in there," he said, pointing at the cupboard. He flicked on the lights. "You have to eat Alex. You're starting to look like a heron."

"Don't mock me. I'm not hungry. Anyway…"

"It's snowing out. Let's eat something. You'll feel invigorated. Then we'll go for a walk. I bought the healthiest stuff I could find." He poured chocolate cereal and milk. He read to her from the side of the box. "It's all healthy."

She poured water into the kettle and rooted through the cupboard for a tea bag. "I'll make tea. Do you want tea?" But she could not find any tea. "I can't even make you a cup of tea."

"Why don't you play?" he said. "Play something."

"I can't," she said. "I've tried." The windows were covered with frost in a crackled star pattern. Something her mom would have crocheted for the holidays. She watched as small birds scattered about the room. Finches fluttered up to the ceiling beams. She ran over to the window, opened the latch to set them free. The birds were perfectly still, resting on the ceiling beams, and not moving to the window. Then suddenly, one after the other, the birds dropped through space, thunking to the floor. She dropped down cradling and patting the air. "Their feathers are falling on me. I must have killed them."

"There's nothing here. You're cold." He lifted her onto the bed, covered her with the quilt and lay down beside her.

"Is that you, Jeremy?" she said, when she opened her eyes. "Do you believe in fate?"

"I don't know, I don't think so. Try to sleep."

She fell asleep again. When she woke, Jeremy was gone. There was light from the streetlamp. Though the window was open only a small crack, the curtains were fluttering. She went to her cello. Once her eyes adjusted to the darkness, she sat on a chair, positioned her back, her feet, and braced her instrument against the floor. She tilted the neck to the left, allowing the instrument to fall into her chest, and took the bow into her hand. Before she could begin, the ribs of her cello started vibrating, moving up and down like waves rolling in. The fingerboard was warm. Dark intonations rose in a whisper. *Lamentoso.* She rested her ear flat over the f-hole trying to hear. *Blackbird singing in the dead of night, take these broken wings and learn to fly.*

After, in bed, she curled herself into a small ball. Her stomach ached and her eyes hurt. People died from the plague before anyone knew they had it. She dreamed of falling. Of the light leaving her. Of being extinguished.

"Do you have a boyfriend Alex-sand-ra?"

"Well, yes, a sort-of boyfriend. A friend really."

"What's his name?"

"Jeremy."

"Jeremy is a nice name."

"Does he play the cello?"

"No." She laughed. "He likes electronic dance music."

"Does he like deadmau5?"

"What? How do you know who that is?"

"Are you going to marry Jeremy?"

Most days Alexandra did not see Jeremy. He was busy with school. He would call. Always urging her into the psychology study.

"I think you're depressed. You should see someone."

"You're in economics, not psychology."

"I don't think it matters. Please."

Was she depressed? How was she supposed to know? Her suitcase was on the floor. Still packed. She was unbearably tired.

"Guess what?" He was suddenly chipper.

"Don't make me guess. I'm no good at guessing."

"For Valentine's I bought two tickets to Yo-Yo-Ma at Roy Thompson Hall," he said.

"You did? You hate classical music."

"I know. I was thinking of you. Why don't you take that kid?"

"Caterina?"

"Yes. Valentine's Day is on a Tuesday evening. I have midterms."

"Really? Do you mean it?"

"Yes, really."

"You're a class act, Jeremy Benson. I've been meaning to tell you that."

At the end of the lesson Alexandra asked Caterina, "Do you want to go to see Yo-Yo Ma with me?"

Caterina flew running out of the room. "Mom!" she hollered as she ran through the house. "Can I go see Yo-Yo Ma with Alexsand-ra?"

"It might be sad," Alexandra said to her. "He's going to be playing a sad piece."

"What kind of a sad piece, Alex-sand-ra?"

"Edward Elgar's 'Cello Concerto in E minor.' For a solo cello."

"I never heard of Edward Elgar. Who is he?"

"Well, he lived in England, a long time ago. He wrote this score after World War I. He was in his home in England, mending."

"Mending? That's a funny word."

"Well, he had been sick. His wife thought if they moved to the country, he would get better."

"Oh," she said. They were sitting on the floor with their knees touching.

"When he would lie in bed, he could hear the sound of fighting, across the water, in France. He said that this piece was about the sadness he felt."

"That's so beautiful."

"Not too sad?"

"I'm not afraid to be sad," Caterina said. "You need sad to find happy."

Alexandra laughed. "Yes, you do."

At 6 p.m. on February 14, Alexandra tiptoed down her tilted stairs. *Moderato.* She turned, walked backwards through the front door, remembered to stop at the garden gate, turned around and made her way to the subway stop. She picked up Caterina, and together they took the subway to Roy Thompson Hall. Caterina was wearing a black wool coat with large shiny black buttons. In her right hand she was clutching a small red purse with an appliqué of a Scottie dog. On her feet she had shiny black shoes with little buckles, and she sparkled from head to toe.

Once they took their seats on the subway, Caterina unzipped her red purse and reached inside. When she opened her hand, she was holding a red foil heart.

"Here," she said. "For my favourite teacher in the whole wide world."

"Thank you," said Alexandra. She pushed the foil heart into the pocket of her down coat.

"No no no," said Caterina, tipping her head to one side, and wagging her finger at Alexandra. "You have to eat your heart. It's good luck when someone gives you a heart."

On the way up to the front entrance of Roy Thompson Hall, Caterina sped up. "Hurry up, Alex-sand-ra," she said. "I don't want to miss anything."

When they took their seats, Caterina opened and began reading her program. "It says, Edward Elgar's 'Cello Concerto in E minor.' And then Intermission. Then, after the Intermission it says 'Simple Gifts.' Arrangement by Aaron Copeland. I don't think that will be sad Alex-sand-ra." She had barely taken a breath.

"Let me see." Alexandra read what was written in the program.

'Tis the gift to be simple, 'tis the gift to be free
'Tis the gift to come down where we ought to be,
And when we find ourselves in the place just right,
'Twill be in the valley of love and delight.
When true simplicity is gain'd,
To bow and to bend we shan't be asham'd,
To turn, turn will be our delight,
Till by turning, turning we come 'round right.

"Well. You're right. Rule number three."

"Yes, Alex-sand-ra. I'm having the most fun in the whole wide world."

Caterina squeezed Alexandra's arm so tight she could feel her blood coursing through her veins. Then something weird. She felt a snap and Mom and Dad's blood was running inside of her too. Systolic and diastolic; thumping and murmuring. Filling and emptying. She could have been mistaken, but there were three sounds. Thumping, murmuring, and whooshing. Strangely comforting. Then the vibrations calmed and disappeared altogether.

As the curtain opened, Alexandra glanced sideways at Caterina. She was sitting perfectly poised in her red velvet dress, with her long red hair tied with a ribbon, and her little red purse with the Scottie dog balanced on her lap. Her eyes were wide as buttons. With one hand she held onto Alexandra's hand. With her free hand, Alexandra unzipped her puffy down coat. She reached into her pocket and felt the crushed pieces of maple leaf and the crumpled red foil. She pulled her hand back out of her pocket and began to unwind her scarf from around her neck. It was warm tonight inside Roy Thompson Hall.

THE RAIN WON'T COME

"Your mother is gone," the voicemail from the caregiver said, like a breeze passing. "Her father has called her home."

My attention leapt to Vancouver and Mother and whether I was feeling loss or reprieve. I walked to the rear of the operating hut and was relieved to find the door unlocked. I could steal several minutes alone before the next surgery. How did the caregiver know about my grandfather? As far as I knew my mother hadn't spoken a word in the last year.

Outside, the clinic was surprisingly quiet. Waiting patients were dozing in the heat of the late afternoon. I looked down at my phone and listened to the message. I envied people who knew exactly what to do. Vancouver was 15,000 kilometres and at least three flights away. Then I drifted upward. The bottom of my feet lifted off the ground and I gazed down at the Tanzanian veld, eucalyptus trees, patches of mangrove forests and rocky pastureland blazing in the sun.

As a child, I was often left alone to look after myself. Needing playmates, I became a daydreamer, frequently floating in a make-believe world. From the day of my fifth birthday when my father collapsed at the table and died, there had been just two of us: my mother, who never stopped calling herself an immigrant, and me, her son, whose job it was to rise in the world. "That's all I ask," she'd say when I was in school. Once she got sick, she would repeat the same three sentences. "My work is finished. You've made me proud. Now I want to go home."

Hearing that voice message hit me hard. I should get on a plane to Vancouver but I'm in rural Tanzania. The airport was a day's drive away in good weather. And rain was on the way. Only this morning, Lotte, our local nurse teased, "It's a good thing you like us here, doctor. Once the rains start, you'll be marooned."

Meanwhile, out the door of the surgery, villagers were lined up through the courtyard, looped around the clinic, sitting, standing and sleeping on the dusty road. I'm confident the line has been like this for the two years I've been working here. Though my Lotte says every day the line keeps growing. All of them waiting for cataract surgery. A simple fifteen-minute operation to restore their sight. They were scared but they came anyway. Yesterday we had a five-year-old boy who was afraid we were going to give him goat's eyes.

I had to get back to the operating hut. Surely this was where Mother would have wanted me to be. For the last year, she'd been lying in bed in a nursing home. All her life a working woman, cleaning up people's unmade beds and dirty toilets. Then she began to whittle away. We didn't talk. She'd stopped talking. She wasn't interested in food either. The sight of her like that unnerved me. The truth is, I hadn't visited her in months. As far as I could tell, if there had been a door she could have pushed open to get the other side, she would have pushed it.

"This is Faraji," Lotte said. "He's been in line for three days. He's sixty-nine years old and a farmer. His son has brought him." With the best of humour, Lotte seemed to do everything imaginable to keep control of the villagers. You can't believe how they pushed their way into the clinic, curious, sticking their noses into everything.

A stooped man with thick greying hair, eyes clouded with a milky sheen and most likely going blind, stepped forward. Good Lord, he was the same age as me. From that small exchange, I guided Faraji to one of the surgical stations. The ceiling fan whirred, and the cool air felt good. I didn't tell him that I was about to make a slit in his eye. I've learned from Lotte not to say anything. They're awake for the procedure and cutting into the body frightened the villagers. Before long Faraji was back on his feet and poking at his bandaged eye. He shook my hand and gestured to his son to hand over a plastic cage with a live chicken. Patients often give gifts, but today I felt unexpectedly moved to tears by his gratitude.

Then I closed up the surgery for the day. It's awkward to leave when the patients don't leave. But appointments don't work. People come when they can leave their crops or when there is someone to accompany them. The lines will be there tomorrow and just as long.

Walking to my room under a star-filled sky I was overcome with loneliness. The air was humid but otherwise I had no sense that rain was on the way. The sun was down and there was a pleasant wind. I opened a cold Serengeti, heated up vegetables and rice, and thought about the chicken I'd left at the hospital. I bet Lotte had taken it home. It wasn't going to be me wringing its neck. I couldn't kill a spider. The wind brought dust through the crack in the shutters. I lay down on my cot and stared up as dust hummed and twirled. In this simple room, I became calm and unhurried and soon fell into a tunnel of sleep.

Crunching through a tiny opening I lowered myself into darkness. I closed my eyes as I somersaulted backwards down through a moss-covered opening in the earth.

I eventually came to a stop on hands and knees at the doorway of the Arbutus Nursing Home. The metal door was so heavy I could barely shove it open. There wasn't much to pack. I hurried to open doors, drawers and cupboards gathering the things of her that remained. I moved quickly. A cupboard filled with old shoes I'd never seen before. Teeth, hearing aids, plastic spoons. The clink of her gold bracelet as it fell to the floor. Her Bible. Inside the cover a faded photograph of her parents holding their first-born son. And on the back, written in script, Celebes, Indonesia and dated 1917. I slid the photograph into my breast pocket. I was told to remove everything. So, I did. I found a housecoat with her name on it, folded in a corner of her cupboard, the colour of a Blush Rose. I had given it to her on Mother's Day. Like new and never worn. I took off down the hall to find someone who might be able to use it. It didn't take long. Joyce in Room 303 took it out of my hand, grinned at me, and shut her door in my face.

Mother's small room grew stifling like the tropics when the rain won't come. I couldn't make the window budge. Mother's bed was a thin mattress stripped now to a plastic cover with a dip in the middle where she used to be. I placed her suitcase by the door and surveyed her room. Then I sat on her bed.

Suddenly and unmistakably, there was Mother propped up on a pillow. The sight of her was terrifying and exciting at the same time. She was wearing a blue and white batik dress exactly like the one her mother wore in the old photograph and her long dark hair pinned up under a woven *cloche,* which made no sense at all. I was like a child seeing my mother dressed for a special outing. She was years younger and deftly slicing a mango in her lap with what looked like a small hunting knife.

She reached across the bed balancing a slice of mango on the knife blade and in the commanding voice I remember from my childhood, said, "This is how fruit should taste, juicy and sweet. Not like the tasteless soggy mush they served in here. And tea so weak it may as well have been dishwater. I'd love a breeze, could you open the window?"

I showed her the photograph.

Then she began speaking as she never spoke before of her past.

"That's your grandparents." I sat on the bed beside her, content to listen.

"Your grandfather died before I was born. Killed by a spear in an uprising where he was working as a missionary. That night my mother escaped through the night on horseback, through the highland jungle on the remote island of Celebes, Indonesia, with two young children, and me in her belly, yet unborn."

Lost in a dream, unaware of the passing of time, I lay breathing in the exotic scent of her. "Where were they?" I asked.

"They were on the veranda of their house of braided palm leaves and bamboo slats, perched on the hill. Almost a year before the uprising. A year before the night of the greatest tropical storm, thunder and lightning that lasted that night and the next day. Such a storm the villagers would later say they had never seen. That was before my father, alone in his hut, sat playing the piano when a man burst in with a spear. Before an oil lamp was knocked to the floor lighting the bamboo walls on fire. Before my father bled to death in his burning house."

She continued with her story, her arms pointing into the space beyond us, as though we were there. Words flowed out of her like a tsunami, wave upon wave.

"I was born two months after he died, in Palopo, a village on the coast. Delivered by someone moored on a ship in the harbour who said he was a medical man. I don't know what day is my birthday. I have no birth certificate and no record of my baptism. My mother was frightened and barely knew what was happening then."

Her voice was eager and melodic. It was gratifying now to hear the stories of her early life. When I was young, I often asked about her family but she would shoo me away. For a school project when I was thirteen, I was assigned to draw our family tree. I chased her from the kitchen to the living room and back again. I set down the first draft and showed it to her. I had drawn a great trunk with many branches. A mighty oak. But there were no leaves, no names. She left the room in tears like I had sliced open a wound. If a door was in reach, she closed it. I blamed the war, her sadness about dad dying, back-breaking work, keeping up our house and the garden. She planted roses in our yard until I could pick them from my third-storey bedroom window where I would sit looking down on her.

"It took my parents more than two months to travel from Rotterdam to Celebes. A place almost unknown in Holland then. When their church asked, they answered. Some people are like that. They barely blink. They go on faith."

The lights were flickering. I wanted to coax her to talk about our life too. I had spent years trying to get away from home. Never seeing that she had travelled far from her home too. But she'd closed her eyes. Her voice was tiny and whispery. "I'm an old woman now and I'm going home."

Home to her meant the place she was born. Place of orchids blooming all year, luscious green hills, jagged volcanic mountains, vast tea plantations and surreal light. And the father she never knew. Fragments of memories filtered through photographs and the suggestions of her imagination.

The air in the tiny room grew warmer. I lowered my head and spoke into her ear. "Now you are preparing to fly home. To the home you barely knew and always longed for."

If I could make wings for her, I would have done it. I stroked her hair. The bright light and vibrant colours of her plumage fluffed, catching balmy pockets of air. Enough to take her where she needed to go. I could see now she was beautiful, wet my finger and wiped a drip of mango from her lips. I lifted her hand, felt for her pulse. I placed my ear to her chest to listen for her heartbeat. Nothing. She flowed away like warmed honey. I brushed her soft papery hand on my cheek. Tiny fragments of skin broke off and fell onto me.

It was 4 a.m. when I woke to my driver knocking at the door of my room. "It's time to go, doctor."

I rose slowly through the darkness, lingering in aromas of tea, cinnamon, frangipani and salt air. And all that had been given.

"We are expecting a thunderstorm. Good to hurry."

Outside rain had started to come in gusts. Palm branches drummed against the windows. The sky blared at the earth like a bugle. The light rattled and flickered. I picked up my suitcase, which was weightless now, as though it were empty. I couldn't leave without opening a window.

Snow Geese

The birds are starting to migrate north, and I am riding
my bike, melancholy of mind, observing scenes of flight.
The line flies together, talking to each other, their black
wings flickering, displacing air. This is the place where
we rode together. A place I wished could go on forever. But I'm older now and alone. I ride on in the dim
hour edged by light and a familiar horizon, watching
the birds flying forward.

"Don't ride over the tiny toads!" he hollered back at me that day.
"The tiny road?" He was riding uphill and I was fifty feet
behind. His words scattered into the bushy thick of the forest.
"Watch where you're going!" He was shrieking, really.
"What?" I shouted. I couldn't for the life of me guess what he
was getting at. My first thought was he'd narrowly missed a ditch
or a new rut in the road and tried to warn me. But then, you never
know what's around the bend. If there was a bear on the trail, he
would be silent and back up slowly. He wasn't one to panic and
yell out. Something was wrong, but I couldn't see that far ahead.

That morning my legs were waltzing pistons, up down,
up down. My blood felt like it was running high-test
gasoline, driving my quads and my calves, powering
my feet, turning the pedals, pushing my bike effortlessly over tree roots, loose rocks, crevices with trickling
streams going downwards while I was going upwards. I
rose effortlessly out of the saddle, climbing. In the zone.

I remember this. A decade ago. The day John died.

I was thinking about the last thing he said as we left the house. Remember—smell, feel, see. I drew air in through my nose. There was the smell of breakfast scones and oil from my bike chain, pine trees, old man's beard draped from the branches, the earth with its scents, holding secrets I'll never know. The touch of sun warming the back of my cycling jersey. Seeing is difficult today, going from light to dark in the woods, my eyes waiting to adjust. I can't keep from looking down at the jagged rocks, gnarly roots, bending slanty turns. The eroding cliff edge. Wander into the mystery. That's what he would say.

My thoughts are an hour down the trail, already at the lookout. I'll stop there; sit on the wooden memorial bench that's perched on a rocky ledge. I will be un-hurried. I will look out onto the valley and the moun-tains and long-legged aspens rising up above the forest now that it was autumn, giddy as bright stars. An en-graved plaque on the bench reads John Whitehead 1958 – 2002. Forty-four years old. When my time comes, I want a bench, beside John's bench. I say a prayer every day, it's true, for finding my other half and that chance had knocked us together into love. And I remember the one thing he said every morning. Don't be in such a hurry.

"Don't ride over the what?" I called out. The sky was bright, I was riding in and out of shadows. Forest to bridge. Wanting to see what he wanted me to see. I jammed the brakes, gave the front brake more squeeze than the rear and narrowly missed ramming into his rear wheel. This was the second time today I'd done that. So many things to think about with this mountain bike he'd bought me.

In one swift movement, he jumped off his bike and slumped to the ground, his bare knees onto the dirt. "Come here, look. Tiny toads. They're no bigger than my palm. Geez, we almost missed seeing them."

As long as I was moving, I was riding like an ace. Weaving through the trees. Now that I'd stopped, I forgot everything, thinking about reeling in my first trout on a fly rod, under my father's tutelage. Keep the pole high, reel slowly, give some slack. Always my nerves would fray. I straddled my bike, held tight to the brakes, and slowly lifted my leg off onto the up-hill pitch. Nothing about this felt natural.

He sprang off of the ground, grabbed hold of my bike and leaned it against a tree. Then dropped to the ground again, pulling me with him until we were side by side crouched facing the gravel and a parade of toads. He was a smiling boy with a bug collection. I couldn't see anything. Then I did. The surface of the dusty trail was weaving, jiggling and dancing. Scores of thumb-size toads were crossing the path like ants, going somewhere, like they had been called to dinner.

"Some of them aren't moving," he said. He glanced sideways at me, his green eyes textured as sphagnum moss. He rubbed his neck with his thumb, a particular way he would press, massaging his muscles, whenever he was nervous. Something just like my dad would do with his hand. Then I'd realize, even if it wasn't obvious, something was bothering him.

Since my dad died, my own nerves have been switched on like a barking dog. The kind of high-pitched nagging noise that made it impossible to focus on anything except my own grief. After the memorial service, Mom said, "You have to work at love. It's not that complicated. That's how it was for your father and me. We didn't take it for granted."

"They're migrating. They're going to lay their eggs. Then they're going to die. Some of them are dead already," he said. He scooped up one of the small toads in his hand. "Oh no, have we been riding over them? Jesus."

"No, I think they're moving," I said. I prodded one of the toads with the tip of my finger. "Some of them are slow, that's all. They're frightened. We're too close. We're breathing on them. Let's move away. See?" I said, as the brown bumpy knot began moving again.

"Don't kiss the frogs," I said, rapping on his shoulder with the tips of my fingers. I was thinking about our relationship and how he always did the most work at love. I was also thinking, he's breathing too hard.

"The princess is supposed to kiss the frog." His jersey was stuck to him like shrink-wrap. Too wet for the short distance we'd ridden, the morning air still cool. We should move on. But we didn't.

He put his finger on my lip, leaned in and kissed me. I started to hum. Humming was code. It meant I like that. The inside of my head was vibrating. We're twins from different mothers, I wanted to say. Like I'd always known him. Both a lover and a friend. Some of us are lucky this way. I linked my hand in his hand. In the last year, since my dad died, I'd changed. There was something in everything that made me sad. I felt so guilty. He'd try to cheer me up, telling stupid jokes, chuckling more than he should.

"Gotta stop," he said, "and gather ye rosebuds. Right?"

"'Gather ye rosebuds while ye may,'" I said, barely above a murmur. "'Old time is still a-flying: And this same flower that smiles today. Tomorrow will be dying.' Can you believe my dad used to recite that poem?" I shrugged. "My dad never stopped to smell a damn thing."

His eyes were back watching the tiny toads make their pilgrimage.

"You're not in a hurry," I heard myself say. I slipped back into watching him.

And then we jumped back on our bikes and carried on, traversed a thicket of Douglas fir and lodgepole pine in silence. I don't know for how long. The trail climbed steeply and then split off and levelled into an undulating single-track switch-backing through the forest. On this ride, we would crisscross a couple of creeks, reach the lookout with views of the valley and loop back descending to the lake and home. Chasing the last streaking light of summer. Crossing a couple of creeks entailed crossing a couple of bridges. I had to push that thought from my mind.

The night before he'd readied our bikes: wiped down the stems and saddles with a rag, checked the tires for air, cleaned old crud off the chains.

"Man, I've wanted to take this ride all month. How did it get to the last day of September? Hope it doesn't rain tomorrow."

I loved the excitement he created. The light in his eyes. Most of all the little details, preparing, the anticipation.

We'd ridden the trail in spring, when the woods were quiet. Then stayed away completely during summer when the tourists came. Clear skies this morning felt like good luck. We had been riding since breakfast. Zigzagging upward from Green Lake, our bike tires gripping gravel still moist with dew, the fog burning off. Halfway across the new Fitz Creek Bridge, he stopped his bike and waited for me. He knew about me and bridges. Once or twice, as we started climbing, when the clang of my changing gears and thump of rubber bouncing over rocks and roots, through trickling streams grew faint, he'd stop again. I knew he didn't mind.

I'm enjoying the solitude of the trail. It's a relief not to have to maneuver my bike to pass other cyclists on the narrow trail. I stay well clear of the jagged rim where there is a long drop off that ends in a ditch. When the trail is busy, I have to swoop around another rider coming towards me, I can't help staring at that ditch until I may as well point my bike straight down the gully, tumble head over handlebars, and get the fall over with. Today the sun is a warm blanket, the trail snaps with dry leaves and pinecones, the canopy of the forest is rising up like a church steeple. What I would say now is that I wished those days could have gone on forever.

My mind curled back to that breakfast and home-made scones with blueberries, poppy seeds, sunflower seeds and chia. Everything he could find in the kitchen cupboard shaken out and stirred into the batter. He made such a racket clanging dishes and banging the cupboard doors, awake at six o'clock, just like my dad. As I descended the stairs, I heard him singing. Good-bye, hasn't been so good to me. He liked to sing. It didn't matter if he was in the shower or cleaning out the gutters.

"What do you like about that song?" I asked.

He filled up the golden oriole mug with coffee, to the brim, no room for milk. "Hot, dark, and sweet, just like me," he said, ignoring my question.

I laughed at his conceit. Except for the way his nose was bent, like it had been welded on, he couldn't be more handsome. His mother told me he'd been hit by a car once, long before I knew him. Broken nose, cracked knee, skin graft on his thigh.

"Don't laugh. I'm serious." I sipped the coffee from the golden oriole. All of our mugs were bird mugs. Rufous hummingbird, bushtit, cedar waxwing, western tanager, Steller's jay, swallow. I'd given him the golden oriole mug on Valentine's stuffed with dark chocolate hearts. A golden oriole is not a western bird. I didn't know that.

"Doesn't matter. All birds are beauties," he'd said.

"That song. It's making you sadder. Is that what you want?"

"Na," he said. "Come on. Sing with me." He took the mug from my hand, set the mug down and pulled me to my feet.

"You're crazy," I said. "I can't sing. I can't dance."

"Why not?"

"I'm not like you."

"It doesn't matter." He swung me around past the open window and back.

"Maybe one day when you choose a happy song," I said.

He turned his back and opened the oven door and pulled out the metal cooking tray. "Hmm. Perfection." He put the tray down and took hold of one of scones, tore it apart with the tips of his fingers.

"'By My Side' is a happy song."

"If you say so." He held the ragged piece of steaming biscuit to my mouth, like a mother bird feeding her hatchlings.

I ducked under low hanging branches and swung around a sharp curve that I'd never negotiated once on this trail without getting off my bike and pushing it around and up the incline. Today my mountain bike was a dance partner leaning into each turn and twisting, each rise and fall. The woody fragrance from pinecones, bark, and needles stirred memories of all the rides we had done together. I tried again to see what lay exactly in front of me. Tried to see naturally, the way he saw. But all I could think about was getting to the lookout and sitting on that bench.

Even on a trail you think you know, there is such a thing as the unexpected. I screwed up my eyes and stopped my bike. A few metres in front were two planks over a narrow gorge. And no railings. I had never seen this bridge before. I stayed put where I had stopped, held my bike upright, my eyes scanned either side of the bridge, looking for an alternate way to cross over. The narrowest point looked to be in front of me. The two planks. I considered walking my bike down the steep bank, traversing the river on foot, and ascending the other side. But the gorge was really just a crack in a slab of rock, too flat, too steep to scramble on foot.

Bridges were like ghosts. My entire life I have been under their spell. I built them with toy blocks when I was three or four years old. From the first day I could hold a crayon I began drawing arching spans onto long sheets of newsprint rolled across the floor of my bedroom. Until I was sent to bed and dreamt of bridges; every kind of span, wood, stone, iron, or steel, meant to carry one safely across a creek, river, strait, or other body of water. I was afraid of real bridges. Often in my dreams I would find myself halfway across, crawling on my hands and knees and would wake up frightened and shaking.

It made logical sense that repeated exposure to bridges should help. But it never did. I could never bury my fear. I was not afraid of falling in, or of getting soaked in the cold water, or drowning. But something I could not describe precisely would bring me to a standstill. Some kind of weakening in me sent my legs wobbling the instant I began across a bridge. My body would sway, my breathing would quicken like an engine choking trying to start up. I would always have a feeling that something terrible was about to happen. Like in the movies, a stick of dynamite blowing the thing to smithereens.

That day I looked down into the gorge. It was like looking down into a well. I couldn't tell if the water was deep. It was certainly black. Goosebumps formed on my arms. Bridges can crumble, splinter into a thousand pieces, snap in half, just like that.

"We're going to cross it together," he said. "Don't look so worried." I startled, jumped. I hadn't seen him. He was leaning on his bike, off to the side of the trail, waiting for me.

"What's up?"

He pulled off his helmet. His hair, standing up, was soaking wet.

"You okay?" I should have been relieved. He would help me across, but he was pale. His eyes didn't look right. I was having trouble reading his expression. Like trying to read a mask, his features erased.

"Just taking in the views," he said, wiping his sunglasses on his shirt. "It's humid."

"No, it's not."

"Did you hear the woodpecker?"

I leaned on my handlebars. "No, where?"

"Back by that cluster of pines. Loud as a steel drum. Like there was a whole band banging out calypso with bamboo sticks." He was breathing fast, speaking in short staccato bursts.

"First pileated woodpecker I've seen this year. I rode right under him and then heard ping, ping, ping. I had a perfect view of the brilliant red head with the white stripe. It could have been pulling on a hockey jersey. Butting its bill into that tree as though it has an entire family to feed."

"I wish I could see the way you see," I said.

"You aren't paying attention."

"You're right. I'm always gone in my own thoughts. Can you imagine if you hadn't come into my life? I'd never get dressed.

Get out the door even. I'd still be at my desk, scratching out draw-
ings from dawn to dusk."

"Someone else would have dragged you out into the world,
don't you think?"

"Look at this," I said, turning to the bridge.

"I thought you might not notice and ride right over."

"Very clever of you. That's not going to happen."

"Ah shoot. You got over the Fitz Bridge no problem at all.
How did you manage that?"

"The Fitz Bridge is about a foot off the ground, the railings
are four feet high, and you can't see through the slats. It barely
qualifies as a bridge at all. These planks are new. Looks like newly planed Douglas fir. What do you think happened to the old
bridge?"

"You're right. I don't know. It's weird. You miss the woodpecker and see the bridge. Like it's a work of art. But then you're
afraid of the work of art too."

"I know. What's wrong with me?"

"Nothing."

"I always feel something bad is going to happen."

"Well, bad things do happen. Not usually. But they do."

"Like my dad dying."

"Want to stop here?"

"Or should we push on?" I asked. "In ten minutes, we could
be at the lookout and rest."

"We'll get to the lookout. I promise we'll stop there. I was
wishing we could stop and talk first. I'd been looking for a grassy
bit. I should have known you'd find a bridge."

"Let's sit on the bridge," I said, pointing to the middle of the
span where the sun overhead had broken through the canopy.

"Really? Are you sure?"

"Yeah. Today's the day."

"You're nuts. But alright."

"I want to do it. I want to sit in the middle of this bridge
until I'm not afraid anymore. Don't wait, right?"

"If you say so." He pulled the water bottle off his bike and
shoved two Clif bars into his pocket.

At the threshold he took hold of my hand. I'd gripped him too tightly, my fingernails digging into him. He said nothing and held onto me. I moved timidly, my legs swinging stiff as a wind-up marching toy. Then I stopped.

"Wait." My feet had fixed to the plank like they'd been glued. I was afraid he would topple off the side taking me with him.

"Look ahead to the other side and don't look down. Look where you're going, where you want to end up. I'll talk to you until we reach the middle. Okay?"

We started again walking hand in hand, arms touching.

"Look where you're going," he said again. "You're looking at your feet."

"Where am I going?"

"You're going home," he said. "Keep walking. Twenty paces and then we'll be in that big puddle of sunlight."

I started to talk, ambling with my nervousness. "Jack McCracken said it helps if you eat something when you're afraid."

"Who's Jack McCracken?"

"The psychologist who writes for the *Times*. He said to eat something sweet. He says you can't be afraid when you're eating something sweet."

"Really? Well, like I said: hot, dark, and sweet. That's me." He squeezed my hand. "You're doing great."

"He meant something sweet, like ice cream."

"A Clif bar?"

"No. Not a Clif bar."

By then we'd reached the middle of the bridge.

"I'm okay."

We sat down in sunshine in the middle of the small span and stripped off our cycling shoes and socks. He dangled his legs over the side. So, I dangled mine. The act seemed effortless. We were quiet then, looking upriver. The woods were remarkably still as though a spell had been cast upon them, as though we'd been sitting on this small bridge our entire lives.

"Bridges might be my totem," I blurted.

"Really? I'm not sure what you mean. Like a spirit guide?"

"I think they're my symbol. Of my tribe. My clan."

He shimmied closer until we were touching, arm to sticky arm. "A bridge is a thing. Can a thing be a totem? Go on."

"I think it's something inside me, the way a river has its own course. Something that takes you where you need to go."

"Bridges?"

"Yeah."

"You're afraid of bridges."

"I know." My mind shot back then to my first memory ever on a bridge. To the long covered wooden bridge in Hartland, New Brunswick.

"I was born within a stone's throw of the Hartland Bridge, and everywhere I go I seem to be confronted by a bridge."

"I forget that. The Hartland Bridge. The longest covered bridge in the world. We never went there."

"No."

"How long is that bridge anyway? That longest covered bridge in the whole wide world?" He was smirking.

"One thousand two hundred and eighty-two feet. Everyone in Hartland knows that detail. I'll tell you something I never told you before. This is one of my very first memories. I was maybe four years old. Alone in the back seat of our Ford wagon. Dad and Mom were in the front. Dad was driving across the Hartland Bridge. And whistling. There was a total darkness inside that bridge. I had fastened my hands onto the door handle, my eyes closed tight. Then dad stopped the car halfway across. 'Wow, isn't this the best?' he said. 'You can't see where we've come from. Can't see where we're going.' I couldn't open my eyes. He started reciting a story from the news. That spring a car had struck a steel straining beam on the bridge, causing the entire deck of the bridge to drop. I was sitting in the rear seat, all these things running through my mind: hurry up, Dad, start the car, someone's going to hit us, we'll slam the side of the bridge, it'll break, we'll fall into the river. Go, Dad. I couldn't make myself say any of it."

"Wow. You should have saved that story until we get off this bridge."

"The Hartland Bridge is a wishing bridge. When you drive across you are supposed to cross your fingers, hold your breath for the whole length of the bridge and make a wish."

"What did you wish for?"

"Nothing. I never made a wish on that bridge. One day I left, drove from Hartland to Halifax, then all the way out west to finish university. And to you."

"A type of wish. Do you want to get going?"

"No. I'm not done."

"Remember all those days going back and forth on the Sydney Harbour ferries with you staring up at ant-sized tourists climbing the Sydney Harbour Bridge? I couldn't get you to walk over it. Even with safety gear. You wouldn't climb it, but you couldn't take your eyes off it."

"I know. I wanted to. I couldn't do it." I leaned forward. Folded my hands beneath my legs on the wooden planks. "The crossing I always remember most vividly is the one over the falls in Clayoquot Sound. A single log draped over a raging chute?"

"Raging chute? I remember a waterfall. Not prone to exaggeration, are you?"

"It was a torrent. We shouldn't have been there. We could barely see where we were going. It was raining by then."

"It wasn't that bad."

"Yes, it was. And what about the Kettle Valley? Remember?" Once I'd started, all crossings were coming back.

"I'd rather not. Everyone was a mile ahead of us by the time I came back for you."

"You always came back."

"Of course, I came back."

"I wanted to be brave but I couldn't move. And those slats. I had no idea they would be so thin. The worse thing was looking down through the holes."

He pulled his legs onto the deck of the bridge. Enjoying our reminiscing.

"You said, 'Don't look down.' I begged you to let me crawl across. Imagine, you started trying to make me laugh. I didn't look down. I walked straight to you."

He pulled off his jersey. The air was cool now that we'd stopped. I lay down, resting my head in his lap. Listened to his heart

béating, *BOOM, boom* rhythm of bongo drums. He was shivering.
"You okay?"

He looked around, pulled off my jersey and smoothed my
hair. His hand moved slowly down my face, registering the secrets of skin, the curve of cheekbones, the round edge of jaw, the
skewed indentation of my neck. "Why did we go to all these places
you were afraid of?"

"I don't know." I said. "Gravitational pull?" Sweat was bead-
ing on his top lip. Neither of us said anything for a while. Taking
in the filtering light dancing through shadow. The sounds of the
woods in its rhythm. The sun moving slowly across the sky.

"What's your totem?" I asked.

He seemed to be in no hurry to answer. A plump bushy-tailed
chipmunk scurried along the rocks astride the bank, chirp chirping like a squealing infant, stopped and looked up at us, then scurried past and up the gnarly side of a tree. He leaned back on his
elbows, gazed down at my face. "I don't know. Maybe I'm a guide.
Can that be a totem?"

"What kind of a guide?"

"A simple guide. I like to take people places they can't go on
their own apparently."

He had been shifting, trying to find comfort on the hard
deck. He turned his face into the sun. "The season's changing. Can
you feel it?"

"A spirit guide?"

"No," he said. "No spirit. That's you. I'm the doubter. Remember?" He kissed my forehead, my neck, my breasts. Dropped
his forehead onto my face. Into my ear. "You're all I need."

The sun had moved across the bridge and a blast of cool air
passed over us. I wanted to pull off my shorts. Then his shorts. But
I was shivering.

"All those things I could never do on my own."

"You wanted to do them. You needed a little prodding. That
was all."

I saw into his face then, taking in every detail of his landscape.
Exploring and discovering every rut. I was feeling giddy. "I kind of
like it on this bridge."

He began to sing. A simple melody.

I sang back in a tiny out-of-tune voice, like a bird answering her mate's call.

We held each other and sang to the trees. Down into the gorge. Up to the sky. I felt free, fearless.

"It's time," I said then. "You're cold."

We rose to our feet, pulled on our jerseys, socks and shoes. I was still humming, so amused, when I heard a thud. He'd collapsed onto to the bridge deck.

"What's happened?"

"I don't know. Lost my balance."

I reached my hand to him like a pulley. He did not seem to notice.

"Probably a stitch." He drove his hand into his chest. "Jesus, I think I'm having a heart attack."

"What? No! You're too young." I began shaking like a dry fir bough in the wind. I started screaming. Calling his name. "What do I do? God, what?"

He adjusted himself, rubbed his hand over the back of his neck. Turned his head towards me and closed his eyes. His face cracked with pain. I prodded my mind. Folded myself over him listened for breathing. He was shivering. I needed a blanket. The wooden planks beneath my feet began tilting. My legs teetered.

"I'm going to lift you up."

"No. You can't. Let me rest. It'll pass, I can tell." He did not open his eyes.

"I can. I'm going to lift you." Mothers can lift a car off a child if they have to. I rammed my arms underneath his back, yanked with all my might, straightened my legs, and hoisted his frame. He was so still. His arms and legs limp as a dangling puppet.

"Talk to me! Talk me across!" I was yelling.

No words came. He wasn't heavy. He was light as a feather. Light as air. Light as a hummingbird.

I turned to face the far side of the bridge. My own heart pounded loud as thunder, ricocheting off the mountain, soaring from treetop to treetop, traversing the valley. I began. Everything shaking, inside and outside. I walked in the direction of the lookout.

In the direction of Green Lake. In the direction of home. Roaring in my ears until I could hear nothing at all, and the world went quiet. Like a soldier, I carried him to the other side.

This is the place where I see a man passing by and shed my clothes, as if it were natural, run down into the gorge, my feet and hands leaf-whelmed and combing in water falls unafraid of the torrent dissolving in dream swimming and a hint of dazzling light I wished could go on forever. The snow geese fly over, the line of the roost squealing and arching, their black wings flickering displacing air, leaves, feathers.

How Did You Get Here?

Somewhere between sleep and waking, a sweet and melodic voice drifted in, warm and unlikely as a Sirocco blowing across these West Highlands of Scotland. Finding my way to that voice was as difficult as threading a needle in the dark, but I gathered what pith I could and pulled myself through the thick fog of my mind.

"How did you get here?"

I forced my eyes open. I was sprawled on my back across the footpath I walk every day, sun in my eyes, rocks, rubble and my rucksack pressed into my spine, along with a fine slice of Angus Campbell's Crowdie cheese and my own homemade oat scones. I'd been looking forward to a nice sit by the river to have my piece. I will have gone and flattened it all now.

Right away my sights settled on a stranger bending over me. Gave me a heck of a start, out here, by myself and all. With the glaring sunlight, all I could make out were two great round eyes fixed on me, like I was something peculiar. I should scream, but I didn't. Who's going to come if I holler? Couldn't even budge old Duncan, my collie, to keep me company this morning, all full of arthritis and slower than a plough now. Just sits on that rug of his all day. Not even the crows can rouse him anymore.

And what was I doing on the ground, listening to this stranger drawing in air through his nose, loud as an east wind, and the smell of him, like something foreign, musky as incense? Next thing I knew I was shaking like them birch leaves when the wind's up.

"Are ye real then?" I said, thinin' to get him to move back.

"Let me help you to your feet, ma'am."

When he bent over me, his long white hair scattered like

weeping branches. Such a large head and his voice barely a whisper. The strangest thing. This was a face that had missed out entirely on the harshness of life. He had none of the skin of our people, cured ruddy red by sun and the harsh winds that sweep 'cross the corries.

"Goodness no." I said and tried to prop myself upright. "I can do it meself?"

"Looks like you fell. I'll help up." He'd gone and stuck his big head right at my ear, like I was deaf or something.

As best I could, I gave him a quick once-over. He was smart-looking, in pressed grey jacket and trousers and fine shoes. Something about his shoes set me a bother though, but with so many things vying for my attention, I couldn't get my thoughts untangled fast enough. Apart from his clothing, he seemed to have a gentle but serious nature.

I got myself lifted a foot or so off the ground and then next thing I knew things started spinning. I fought like the dickens to focus my eyes proper, but everything was swirling. Then I saw sunlight filtering through new leaf on the birches alongside the river. It lit his face and made him seem kindly. The wild beating of my heart began to quiet, and I felt unafraid of him again. The light rendered him harmless-seeming, and I trust the light. This was the strangest thing, but I wanted this fellow to put his head back next to mine. I had the urge to smell the sweetness of him some more. Behind me I could hear water rushing. I'd gone and fallen on the brae as I made my way down to the flats by the river. That'd be what's happened. I was certain of it.

"I was passing by and saw you. I wanted to make sure you were all right."

Wasn't he well bred? I was looking into the most stunning blue eyes I think I'd ever seen. I felt myself drawn to him, like he was kin. He looked harmless. I wanted to run my fingers over those smooth cheeks. I don't care if I should or I shouldn't.

Then straight as an arrow my thoughts went to my house and the farm. Duncan's counting on me for his dinner and there's chores to be done; beans soaking for my soup, and a pudding to make before the ladies come around on Tuesday. Out of the corner of my eye I saw my walking stick, my good hand still clutching it to my side. Thank goodness.

Lord, what had come over me? This here a perfect stranger and me flat on my back. I remembered starting out, the morning glorious. After all the rain the bluebells were dazzling, tall and thick and opening their wee small heads reaching to the sky. Only a week or so ago this earth had been hard as iron. It seemed spring would never come.

He leaned back on his heels, staring at me, but not budging. Funny, those shoes of his, shiny new, like they'd never been walked in. I caught him taking note of the full length of me too and it was getting me a little self-conscious. I couldn't rid myself of the need to settle who he was. Around here I knew most folks.

I watched him rocking back and forth on those fine city shoes. Not a soul in these parts with shoes like that. Nothing under there to grip anything. And where's his hat? No one fair as him should be walking in this harsh sun without his head covered.

"I've loosened your sweater from around your neck and let me remove your rucksack too."

Who was he anyway, thinking he could take over like that? I spotted a large rock in front of me. I'll brace my stick against it and get myself hauled up. Shoo him off. Then I'll be right as rain. But before I could even get myself going, he lifted me to my feet. I dug my stick into the dirt and waved him on his way.

"You're hurt?" he persisted, not letting go of me. I should have broke free of him, right then. Where was his rucksack? Can't go for a walk way out here without bringing your things, food and such. My belly was heating up like a stoked fire. Good Lord, what was happening to me? I babbled away to take my mind off of the pain, when I should have been biting my tongue.

"I was walking, after me chores. I crossed over my neighbour's croft, took the footpath through the woods, and then I was coming down to the river here."

Then I went quiet. The ache in my belly growing into something fierce. I forced my fist into the hurt to keep it from getting the better of me. The sun was moving overhead. How long had I been lying down?

"Let me help," he said, still holding me upright, my head barely up to his shoulder.

I wanted none of it. I looked up straight into those oversize eyes of his, signalling him to let go of me. Sometimes you don't want softness. The body craves harshness: cold bracing wind, our tough rocky land, the rub of rough woollens. I wanted to be alone. I wanted my morning back. I wanted to go home. I could see the summit of Ben Nevis. Birds were singing. What were they? I know these things. Walked here my whole life. My Alistair climbed Ben Nevis when he was young, right to her summit. Climbed every one of the peaks on this island before we settled here. Now he's gone, a wee speck tucking into one of old Ben's craggy folds is how I see it. And one day I'm going there too. But I don't decide these things, do I?

"Thanking you for your help, now I'll bid ye adieu," I said, with all the authority I could muster, and I moved away from him. Soon as I took that first step pain went through me like lightning.

"I want to go home," I said, pleading like a child.

"You're bleeding." He was all business now. "You need help. Lean into me."

So, I did. I let him hold me, goodness he could have held up a whole house with those arms of his. I needed water. Would he bring some? I could feel the bottom half of my blouse wet with blood, but funnily, I looked away, retracing my steps uphill. My stick fell to the ground and it was all I could do to reach down after it.

This stick of mine, it was the only thing I had from Alistair's hand. He'd sent down south for the wood. You couldn't get cherry here in the north. Didn't breathe a word of it. He never spoke the words of love; locked up whenever he tried. This worn-out old piece of wood wasn't him, but the thought of losing it filled me with a terror. Far off in the distance someone was speaking. I strained but couldn't make out a word.

"You fainted and you're bleeding. I'm going to carry you."

My mind was dreamy like the drink gone to my head. I couldn't think for the minute where my home was. Then, all of a sudden, as though a storm had lifted in me, I knew exactly where I was.

"I slipped on the brae, clear into that spiky, tough marquise there, alongside the path. I rolled myself off of it, and ended up here, flat on my back."

I had been singing. "Unto the hills, the psalm, around do I lift up, my longing eyes." I didn't tell him that. It was what Alistair used to sing when we walked. "Oh, whence for me, shall my salvation come?" His sweet tenor rising up over these hills. Lord, I miss him. It was a loss that abides. I know they say that in time these terrible memories fade and the losses lessen, but that hadn't been my experience. I stopped going to church. It was all tea and cakes and sorry for your loss Mrs. MacKay. None of it helped. I needed someone to hold me during those awful long nights, to tell me that God loved me still. No one did.

Wasn't it just the other night I was sitting by the fire, thinking too much, and rocking myself into a right angry state, when I heard Alistair talking to me like he was in the room? Gave me a start. "Now Isla MacKay, stop feeling sorry for yourself." That was himself alright. There's no mistaking a Hebridean. Always offering up forgiveness like it was a cup of sugar. "You're just too damn proud." Well, I don't know. Seems to me there wasn't a single one of them ladies came 'round when I was sitting by myself, taking my tea all alone. "God's not angry with you. Don't get yourself a hard heart. Do you no good."

I believe I'm going to cry. "You'll be thinking me sentimental now." I had to say something. Like he could hear clear into my thoughts. "Truth is our people are strong. 'Tis what we're known for. I'll make up a poultice soon as I'm home, get myself to right." Despite the warm sun, I was drenched and chittery.

"Listen," he said, and with one of his massive arms folding me into his shoulder. "I've come from across the river. We'll go back across together. I'll find help for you on the other side."

Those words of his were like a knife straight through me. Far more frightening than the wound already in my belly. Was this it then? I looked up, meaning to look into his face, but instead I took in the light. The sky was the deepest blue I'd ever seen.

"I'll not go there." I said to him, maybe three times or four, until I heard myself shouting. With all my strength, I pushed him away. In his face I couldn't see if he was for or against me. "I've walked alongside this river my whole life. You can see for yourself, it's a raging torrent, fraught with whirlpools and eddies, currents what will drag you under. It isn't possible to cross this river on foot. 'Tis much deeper than it looks to the eye. Only a fool would set out to cross it. I don't believe you."

"No," he started. "Please."

I kept talking like my life depended on it. "I come from the Cairngorms. Born here and I'll be buried here too, beside my Alistair, and Duncan too when his time comes. They're inside me, these old blue hills. I'll drag myself home on me hands and knees, but I'll not cross that river. I've got my sheep to attend to and my house and the garden."

Then I went down; tumbling over my stick, face first, onto the stony ground. When I came to, he was stroking my forehead. No one has touched me in such a long time.

"Look, the sun is low, and it will soon be dark. It is too late to start out on a long trail now. You are too weak."

I couldn't quite force my eyes open, but I had to speak up, didn't I? "Don't be ridiculous. We've plenty of time before the sun goes down and I know the way like the back of me hand." Our time on this earth is but a brief moment.

"If that's what you wish, but I'll carry you," he said, and slid both of his arms under me and pulled himself upright, all seeming without effort.

The sun was beginning its descent and I wished for my wool hat and gloves to ward off the cold air.

"That's it for the river, then?"

He started up the trail and didn't answer. I could feel my heart beating everywhere: under my sticky wet blouse, out my toes, and the top of my head. All I could think to do was close my eyes and pray.

The stranger stopped suddenly and turned to the east. He didn't speak but I knew he meant me to look. There across the craggy peak of Ben Nevis a blazing fiery band of red light had set her snowy summit aglow. The light was so astonishing I could barely breathe.

"You're not a monk, are you?" I asked.

"No," he said, "I'm not."

"And your shoes. You're not a walker either."

"No."

"But you're taking me home?"

"Yes," he said, "I'm taking you home."

He carried me in silence as the sky darkened. I wanted to know more of him. How did he get here? I didn't ask. After all, he was taking me home. He seemed to know the way. I grabbed hold of the tip of my walking stick, balancing it as best I could at my side, my thumb going back and forth over the worn knob of the handle.

"Look up, there are two herons."

"No," he said. "Those are crows."

"No, those are herons."

The New Dinner

This winter was all about escape. If it weren't for the rented mountain cabin, the sigh of the north wind funnelling through the valley at night, feeling our teeth chattering in the backcountry woods, and the heat off that Rumford stove, I'm not sure what I would have done. I was coming unravelled, trying to reach back to a yesterday now gone, hoping that having a reason to get out of the city might awaken a new day to take shape. If such a day could.

I'd taken a month off work, and on a Friday evening in mid-February, my husband Nate and I and our Jack Russell, Milo, left the city. Nate and I talked for a while, but he soon fell asleep, his gaunt body curled on the car seat and his head tucked in like a swan. His handsome face returned to him as he slept. I felt for his hand which was pulsating like an electrical current. I let it go. Milo was curled up in the back, snoring, as I drove, ascending, my ears popping with the elevation. Lulled by the quiet and the winding highway, my eyelids were soon dropping too, so I listened to a podcast.

The one that came on was an interview with Laurie Anderson, author of *All the Things I Lost in the Flood*; her cadenced dramatic tone—it was like she was talking and breathing in the car beside me. Describing how during Hurricane Sandy the rising Hudson River was like a living thing, coming up her street in New York City, filling her basement with seawater. All of her musical archives, instruments, and electronics, papers and musical scores had been ruined. Not just ruined, but turned to oatmeal, she said. Everything gone.

I could see all that we owned too turned to porridge pouring out through the windows of our house. Every day Nate was more gone. More thin and more worn. He'd push himself to walk every morning, but he was sipping at the life he used to have. After his walks, he slept. He was all nerves too about spending a month in the woods this time of year. "Where will I walk, Amy?" and "I don't want you to get stuck shovelling the snow."

But we took to that little cabin and as our days formed themselves it became home. Nate found things he could do, making a ritual of building the fire, scaffolding old poles to create a drying rack for our coats and gloves, and rolling up the carpet he kept tripping over. As it turned out, the snow was dry, and Nate's bulky old hiking boots did a terrific job of keeping him from slipping. He never had to shovel the snow once.

By late afternoons, his energy would wane, we'd sit inside and watch the fire. We played board games and read through old *New Yorkers*, sharing stories about palm readers and identical twins and the Birdman of Brooklyn. Nate broke bread crusts into small pieces to feed the Steller's jays. Soon they came looking for him; landing on the deck, squawking loudly, shook, shook, shook, if he missed a meal.

I found an impressive Dutch oven, black as a bowling ball, and at first, I made great batches of winter stews on the Rumford. I invited friends and family from the city, imagining nights of conversation and laughter around a log fire in the cozy cabin. But no one came. It seemed all of them were heading south for the winter. Soon we were content with crackers and cheese and a glass of wine for dinner and our own company. It was a solid little wood A-frame with small windows that were jammed shut. They didn't let much light in, but nothing could flow out of them either.

Every morning, I woke in the dark and tiptoed outside before dawn to watch the day's light arrive over the mountain. In those small moments, the world was perfect sweet silence. I'd steal past the dim flicker of stars and open my mouth to collect snowflakes falling into me like a lost river. I felt free and found comfort in everyday things I had not known since I was young.

By the time Nate woke, the sun was well over the mountain and he'd point out the day's light drenching the mountaintop as if we'd never seen a mountain before. I had a notion of what he was doing. He knew he would soon be leaving. He wasn't one to explain everything he felt. He wanted to restore some small romance; the feelings we had watching morning light. We might never see that kind of light again.

At the end of the month we made the drive back to the city, arriving to a cold empty house, with just enough energy left to empty the car of backpacks, laptops, books and Milo. Too tired to make a proper dinner. It had become easy to overlook the evening meal when there were just two of us. We decided to throw together bits of things, whatever might be left over from the holiday and call it dinner.

It was the first day of spring and the sky was light when we pulled into our driveway. Nate insisted on single-handedly hauling our gear from the garage to the back door, his act of rebellion now. Not so long ago we would have shared the task. I found it almost impossible to watch him carrying the bags, his one leg swinging out like a pendulum, fearing he would trip and fall on his face, break his wrist, or worse, bash his head on the paving stones. But I held back. "Well done," I said as he clumsily opened the back door and dropped everything to the floor, including himself.

Our eyes met then, and he said, "I'm going to lie down before dinner. That drive was exhausting." But Nate wasn't driving. He doesn't drive anymore. Not since his brain surgery last fall. Deep rods were drilled through his skull sending in electricity like bellows, stimulating circuits that had stopped firing. No one told us what to expect. It's not a cure, his surgeon said, but it should give him some mobility. For a while. I knew time wasn't on our side and I suppose they're afraid to get your hopes too high. But since his surgery, Nate started to walk without a cane, and when we were in the mountains, he wanted to try cross-country skiing again. He wobbled in and out of the ski track, his arms tilting like the sails of a windmill. I wished for him that he could ski as he could before but didn't say so.

"Let's go around the track a second time!" he shouted. His slim body teetering, and his knuckles gripping his ski poles. His eagerness. His smile. It wasn't what I had expected.

On the short walk from the car to the back door of our house, I surveyed the garden, surprised to see tiny buds and sprouts

coming to life. Before we'd left for the mountains the earth had
been hard and impenetrable. Now leaves brightened the backyard. Without thinking about all there was to do in the house, I
returned to the garage for a rake. I'd forgotten how fond I was of
going to the garden after work, finishing my day by weeding, snip-
ping and tilling the soil. Milo needed no invitation, he was already
exploring, smelling, chasing scents of mice or city rats, squirrels
perhaps, his nose wedged under the fence looking for intruders
who had passed through while we'd been away. Even before I
turned the earth, I caught myself naming things: air, wind, breath,
space. Things I could not see.

That image of Nate shuffling with the bags brought back a
memory of the dream I had the night before. There was a figure
walking on flat savannah, drenched in light and clutching a battered suitcase. The kind of mythical scene where grasses part and
form a thin dustbowl of a road, no beginning or end. The walker
reminded me of a drifter, going nowhere in particular; his ragged
and ill-fitting clothing picked up at the last camp perhaps where
he'd stopped for the night. As he came closer, I was seized by his
green eyes, Nate's eyes. I was bothered then to see him dragging
one leg noisily down the road. But he went by me with a dignity
as though the parched grassland was what he knew. As though
we'd never known each other at all.

I snapped off dead branches and shrivelled blackened leaves
and asked the garden to swallow me. I raked the topsoil for an hour
like I was working a backhoe, digging in the dirt, scraping twigs
and downed branches.

Soon I began conducting other thoughts in my head; won-
dering about our niece who just dropped out of college, how I
should be calling my office and which of my library books was
due. April was tax month and I hadn't even begun. Chattering
voices of people walking through the alley leaked in through the
fence spaces. A ray of light broke through then and something un-
seeable passed in front of me. I knew by the sudden shock of cool
air. I had an urge to run into the alley to join the strangers walking
by. I leaned on the rake and waited for my breathing to calm and
wished there was someone to tell.

I heard Nate calling from the back door, "Stop raking! You should be resting." But of course, Nate was asleep.

You can't be sure of anything, but the experience slowed my pace and I began to notice details the way monks say when you sweep your garden, you are sweeping your mind. As I pulled the rake through the groundcover and around the paving stones, I stopped to survey the borders, the fence that needed fixing, hellebores flopping on rotted staking, decaying burlap from tree roots exposed through the surface. I bent to pull out little weeds and could see the garden was literally riddled with evolving newness. "Ha," I said, grazing my hand over small coral buds on a maple. "Why did I leave you?"

A northern flicker landed on the fence post. Little finches flitted among the bushes with their sharp high-pitched chirp. Other birds too, that I could not name. While I had been away in the mountains, I'd forgotten that only two hours south, birds would be returning.

But the earth forms and takes. Nate was going. But going where? Into the sky like geese taking off when Milo chased them across the fields? Like the trumpeter swans we'd seen days ago land on an icy mountain lake, stopping briefly on their way to the far north? Like those rare days when Nate and I would be out walking and see an eagle flying and I'd cry out, "Look, right there, right over our heads!" As if we'd been shown a glimpse into something unknown.

I raked and pulled, piled and sorted a layer of detritus as the late afternoon light scattered through the trees. Drawing the long wooden handle of the rake became rhythmic and meditative, and I caught myself humming with memories. Reaching back to walks we had done, our travels, friends, our having been somewhere.

I was getting warm and laid down the rake and unzipped my puffy jacket. Before I could get back to my raking there was a knocking at the gate.

"Aunty Amy, it's us, Jake and Alex." My nephew and his girlfriend. We hugged and they lingered for a while. Jake towered over me and I wondered how it happened so fast. I remembered the day he was born. Alex was tall, too, and with her black trench coat and boots with pointed toes, she was statuesque like a model. So young and exciting looking and I could see how the whole circle starts over again.

When Nate was first diagnosed, our siblings were like first responders. Everyone showed up and poured out love, with poetry, songs written and sung, conversations made over tea and sweets piled high. Expecting he wouldn't last the year. But he did, and now no one came. People were busy. Texts were returned: *I'm writing a term paper, I'll get back to you. I have friends over right now, talk soon.* Some were not answered at all. Quiet arrived in me like a frozen river. Mine alone. I stared up at Jake and Alex. Leaves crackled under our feet as we talked and laughed. I'd completely forgotten that I'd invited them over. It was more than a month ago.

There was almost no food in our house. As if he'd read my mind, Jake swung his pack from his back. "We've brought wine and Camembert and crackers and sausages to slice."

"Come in," I pointed to the couch. "Sit, while I wash up."

Once inside, I pretended not to see the mess our house had become. Belongings piled up at the back door. Milo's blankets draped over the couch and chairs. I imagined the lettuce greens in the cooler wilting. Nate asleep. We had visitors so seldom. Before I'd even turned around, Jake and Alex had taken off their shoes and followed me into the kitchen.

"We'll put together our appetizer," said Jake, as if he could see by the hour and the empty kitchen the job needed doing. I didn't dare refuse. As they entered the kitchen the room took on a warm glow. It felt lively again. Jake swung Alex around, kissed her ear and emptied the contents of his backpack. I noticed I was humming.

And someone else was knocking. Through the glass door, I saw my neighbor Jola with her little boy Wynn. "Our toilet isn't working. Sorry, Amy, can we use your toilet?"

"Of course." I pointed to the bathroom, though she knew where it was. Then I asked her to stay for dinner.

It was only a month we were away. But I couldn't remember if there was wine or some nuts to serve. I opened the fridge and found applesauce and chutney. I rummaged through the cooler; deftly pulling old leaves off the lettuce. Slicing off the hardened edge of a chunk of Jarlsberg cheese. Relieved to see I had packed olives and a jar of artichokes. I remembered the two apples in my purse. Things found in surprising places.

There was someone knocking at the door again. How was it possible that Nate was still sleeping?

"Sorry, Amy, Wynn dumped the cat's water dish."

We don't have a cat. Milo was sitting patiently at the transition between the kitchen and the entryway, a signal that he was ready for his dinner. But Jola is a cat person and thinks all people should have a cat.

Meanwhile, there was my friend Nancy calling from the front door, "I saw your light on and wondered if you would like some of Guy's smoked salmon. Did you just get in? How was your holiday?"

The rule at our house was knock and let yourself in. She waved hello to Jake and Alex, glanced at me opening and closing the doors of the kitchen cupboards and was soon on her phone to Guy. "Bring those little boxes in the fridge from my foraging course yesterday, and a tin of smoked salmon."

"Stay," I said to Nancy. "Stay and eat with us."

I don't know what I was doing, inviting people for dinner. Too much of the lettuce was wilted. There was a too small piece of cheese. And nothing sweet to serve either.

"Do you have a t-shirt I can borrow for Wynn? He's soaked his."

"Yes," I said, unzipping my still-packed bag.

Then Guy arrived at the backdoor with wine and small cardboard boxes, which Nancy took and emptied onto the countertop. Dark green stinging nettles, shiitake, and enoki mushrooms and a bag of large portobellos. "I'm going to make mushroom scallops." I had no idea, but Nancy could transform almost anything into something.

It's terrific how some people take over. They see you need help and jump in. The way I remembered my mother's friends had been. When someone was sick, they'd have brought a casserole. No one asked if you wanted to be alone with your grief. Who in their right mind would want to be alone?

I rifled through my clothes to find a dry t-shirt for Wynn, when I heard *clump thud, clump thud*, on the stairs. Nate was awake and shuffling his way to the kitchen.

The buzz in the kitchen had gotten lively. Good Lord, Jake was playing music on a tiny speaker he'd hooked up on the counter and he was dancing like he was at a street party. Under Nancy's tutelage, Jola was punching out holes in the mushrooms with a cookie cutter, like she was punching out a sheet of paper. Flames flashed from the frying pan. Guy was polishing wine glasses with a ragged linen cloth and holding each one up to the light for inspection. Alex was on the floor with Wynn and clucking like a hen. "And what animal makes this sound?" The room was sizzling beyond my comprehension. If Nate were his old self, he'd have been in the middle of things, uncorking a good red wine, looking for a decanter. Whistling like a winter wren.

"Say hello to our dinner guests," I said.

"Okay," Nate said simply. He was smiling but I saw the hesitation. He was often overwhelmed by having guests now and didn't like surprises. But perhaps I was wrong. "I'll set the table," he said eagerly. "Forks to the right and knives to the left?" he asked, as he swooped and plunked the silverware down. I stood beside him transfixed by his hands trembling as he circled the table arranging forks and knives, plates and glasses, napkins and candleholders with his own choreography. At the places he chose as he brought the table into existence. Table was family to me. I didn't change a thing. I went back to the garden for a handful of thyme and placed a sprig at each place. For courage. Then I closed the windows to keep all the goodness safe inside. I called out everyone's name and turned off the lights.

As though swept along by a current we were soon eight people taking a place around the dining table. I lit eight candles, one for each of us. Light reflected at just the right angle to see all the faces flickering in the near dark. I took Nate's hand and Wynn's small fist, and so on until we were all holding hands. Nate's tight grip was an uncontrollably oscillating voltage that could break up ice on a river. I liked how it felt. Milo took his place at our feet and waited for something to fall from the table. Soon we were chattering, joyously unaware of the passing time, the weeping cool air, the long shadows falling.

Outside, in the garden, the trees and shrubs, flickers and finches, insects and weeds, were shaping their own dialogues.

ACKNOWLEDGEMENTS

To the writers upstairs, who came before. And to the many who have been my particular guides and teachers. Beginning with the audacious, Miss Fluelling, who rang the writer's bell for me back in high school.

A special thanks to my first readers, the writers of the Vicious Circle—Stella Harvey, Katherine Fawcett, Sara Leach, Libby McKeever, Sue Oakey, Nancy Routley, Rebecca Wood Barrett.

Thanks to the good fortunes that brought me to Vici Johnstone and her hardworking crew at Caitlin Press. I have been shown a wisdom and support I had not dreamed of.

Thanks to my editor, novelist and poet, Arleen Paré, who read the work with head and heart.

To Ray, for enduring love.

And to Whistler, place of my belonging.

ABOUT THE AUTHOR

Mary MacDonald is a poet and writer and holds a PhD from the University of British Columbia. She has written poetry for ballet, public art, and libretto. Her fiction has appeared in *Room* magazine and nonfiction in *Pique* newsmagazine. Her chapbook, *Going in Now*, was published in 2014 by NIB Publishing. She is a member of the Whistler, BC, writing group, The Vicious Circle, sits on the board of the Whistler Writers Festival, and serves as curator and moderator for the poetry division of the festival.

The Crooked Thing was typeset with Bembo, a serif typeface created in 1928–1929 by the British branch of the Monotype Corporation. It is a member of the "old-style" of serif fonts, with its regular or roman style based on a design cut around 1495 by Francesco Griffo for Venetian printer Aldus Manutius, sometimes generically called the "Aldine roman." (Wikipedia)